SIX WOMEN

VICTORIA CROSS

1st WORLD
LIBRARY
Literary Society

Six Women

Victoria Cross

© 1st World Library – Literary Society, 2006
PO Box 2211
Fairfield, IA 52556
www.1stworldlibrary.org
First Edition

LCCN: 2006930804

Softcover ISBN: 1-4218-2205-9
Hardcover ISBN: 1-4218-2105-2
eBook ISBN: 1-4218-2305-5

Purchase *"Six Women"*
as a traditional bound book at:
www.1stWorldLibrary.org/purchase.asp?ISBN=1-4218-2205-9

1st World Library Literary Society is a nonprofit
organization dedicated to promoting literacy by:

- Creating a free internet library accessible from any
computer worldwide.
- Hosting writing competitions and offering book
publishing scholarships.

**Readers interested in supporting literacy
through sponsorship, donations or
membership please contact:
literacy@1stworldlibrary.org
Check us out at: www.1stworldlibrary.ORG
and start downloading free ebooks today.**

Six Women
contributed by Tim, Ed & Rodney
in support of
1st World Library Literary Society

DEDICATED TO

H.M.G. AND E.F.C.

AND OUR MEMORIES OF THE EAST.

I

CHAPTER I

Listless and despondent, feeling that he hated everything in life, Hamilton walked slowly down the street. The air was heavy, and the sun beat down furiously on the yellow cotton awnings stretched over his head. Clouds of dust rose in the roadway as the white bullocks shuffled along, drawing their creaking wooden carts, and swarms of flies buzzed noisily in the yellow, dusty sunshine. Hamilton went on aimlessly; he was hot, he was tired, his eyes and head ached, he was thirsty; but all these disagreeable sensations were nothing beside the intense mental nausea that filled him, a nausea of life. It rose up in and pervaded him, uncontrollable as a physical malady. In vain he called upon his philosophy; he had practised it so long that it was worn out. Like an old mantle from the shoulders, it fell from him in rags, and he was glad. He felt he hated his philosophy only less than he hated life - hated, yet desired as the man hates a mistress he covets, and has never yet possessed. "Never had anything, never done anything, never felt anything decent yet," he mused.

He was an exceptionally handsome and attractive individual, and though in reality forty years of age, he had the figure, the look, and air of twenty-eight. Masses of black hair, without a white thread, waved above a beautifully-cut and modelled face, of which the clear bronze skin, with its warm colour in the cheeks, was not the least striking feature. He was about six feet or a little over in height, and had a wonderfully lithe, well-knit figure, and a carriage full of grace and dignity. A bright, charming smile that came easily to his face, and an air of absolute unconsciousness of his own good looks, completed the armoury of weapons Venus had endowed him with for breaking hearts. But Hamilton neglected his vocation: he broke none. He got up early, and slaved away at his duties for the Indian Civil Government in his office all day, and went to bed dead tired at night, with nothing but a dreary consciousness of duty done and more duty waiting for him the following day, as a sleeping companion.

Hamilton's life had been ruined by an early and an unsuccessful marriage. At twenty, when full of the early, divine fires of life, he had married a girl of his own age and rank, dazzled by the beauty she then, in his eyes, possessed, and in that amazing blindness to character that make women view men with wondering contempt. His blindness, however, ended with the ceremony. On his wedding-night the woman, who, it must be admitted, had acted her part of loving submissiveness, of gentle devotion, admirably, mocked at him and his genuine, ardent passion.

How well he had always remembered her words to him as they stood face to face in the chilly whiteness of an English bridal chamber in midwinter! "It's no use, dear, I don't want any of this sort of thing. It seems to me coarse and stupid, and I don't want the bother of a dozen babies. I married because I wanted the position of a married woman, and a nice presentable man to go about with in society. Besides, things were not satisfactory at home, and I wanted a man to keep me, and all that. But I don't see why you should get into such a state of mind about it. I will keep house, and be perfectly good and amiable, and we can go about together, of course; only I want to keep my own room."

And how well he remembered her as she stood there, shattering his life with her cold, light words - a tall, slim girl, in her white dinner dress! She had been very fair then, with a quantity of soft flaxen hair, which shortly after she had taken to dyeing - a thing he had always hated. She had a small, heart-shaped face, so light in colour as to suggest anaemia, with a high, thin nose, of which the nostrils were excessively pinched together, a short upper lip, and a thick, quite colourless mouth, small when closed, when she laughed opening wide far back to her throat, showing, as it seemed, an infinite quantity of long, narrow, white, wolf-like teeth.

How hideous she had suddenly appeared to him in those moments, seen through the dark waves of passion she rolled back upon him! In the hot, rosy glow she had deliberately conjured up before his eyes of love and love returned he had thought her beautiful. Now, as she took the veil from her mean, base mind, it fell also from her beauty, and he saw her ugly, as she really was, body and soul. Stunned and amazed, loathing his own folly, his own blindness, condemning these more than he did her cruelty, Hamilton had listened in silence while she revealed herself. When the first shock was over, he had set himself to talk and reason with her. Naturally intensely kind and sympathetic, it was easy for him to see another's view, to put himself in another's place. He blamed himself at once, more than her, for the position he now found himself in. And patiently he tried to understand it, to find the clue, if possible, to remedy it. He reasoned long and gently with her, but she, knowing well the generous nature she had to deal with, yielded not an inch. Hamilton was not the man to use force or violence. The passions of the body, divested of their soul, were nothing to him. On that night she struck down within him all desire for or interest in her. He left her at last, and withdrew to another room, where he sat through the remaining hours of the night, looking into the face of his future.

Shortly after, he had left for India, the corpse of dead passion within his breast. He made a confident of no one, told no one of his secret burden, remitted half his pay regularly to his wife with that obedience to custom and duty as the world sees it, with that quiet dutifulness that is so astounding to the onlooker, but characteristic of so many Englishmen, and threw himself into his work, avoiding women and personal relations with them.

Such a life as this invariably calls down the anger of Venus, and Hamilton had worn out by now the patience of the goddess.

The tragedy of Euripides' Hippolytus is called a myth, but that same tragedy is played out over and over again, year by year, in all time, and is as true now as it was then. The slighted goddess takes her revenge at last. As he walked on, the sound of some tom-toms dulled by distance came to his ears. He hesitated at a crossing where a side alley led down towards the bazaar, then without thought or intention walked down the turning, the music growing louder as he advanced.

It came from a house some way lower down, before the open door of which hung a large white sheet with scarlet letters on it. Hamilton glanced up and read on it, "Dancing girls from the Deccan. Admission, six annas. Walk in." He stared dully at it till the red letters danced in the fierce, torrid sunlight, and the flies, finding him standing motionless, came thickly round his face. A puff of hot wind blew down the street, bringing the dust: it lifted a corner of the sheet and turned it back from the doorway. Within looked cool and dark. The entry was a square of darkness. He was tired of the sun, the heat, the noise, the dust and the flies. With no thought other than seeking for shelter, he stepped behind the sheet and was in the darkness; a turnstile barred his way: on the top of it he laid down his six annas, his eyes too full of the yellow glare of the outside to see whom he paid: he felt the turnstile yield, and stumbled on in the obscurity. A hand pushed him between two curtains. Then he found himself in a low square room, and could see about him again by the subdued light of oil lamps fixed against the wall. At one end was the small stage, its scarlet curtain now down; in front a row of tin lamps, primitive footlights, and the rest of the room was filled with rows of empty chairs. Mechanically and without interest, Hamilton went forward and seated himself in the first of these rows. The tom-toms had ceased: there was quiet, an interval of rest presumably for the dancers. It was far cooler than outside, and Hamilton breathed a sigh of relief as he sank into his seat. The dimness of the light, the quiet, the coolness all pleased him: he had not known till he sat down how tired he was. He might have sat there a quarter of an hour, his mind in that state of hopeless blank that supervenes on overmuch unsatisfactory thinking, when suddenly the tom-toms started up again with a terrific rattle, and the scarlet curtain was somewhat spasmodically jerked up, displaying a semicircle of girls seated on European chairs facing the tin lamps. Two of the seven were African girls, with the woolly hair and jet black skin of their race; they were seated one at each end of the semicircle, dressed in short scarlet skirts, standing out from their waist in English ballet-girl fashion, the upper part of their bodies bare, except for the masses of coloured glass necklaces covering their breast from throat to waist. The next pair of girls seemed to represent Spanish dancers, and were in ankle-long black and yellow dresses, little yellow caps with bells depending from them sat in amongst their masses of black hair, and they held languidly to their sides their tambourines and castenets. Next on the chairs sat two strictly Eastern dancers in transparent pale green gauzy clothing held into waist and each ankle by jeweled bands. Their pale ivory bodies shone through the filmy green muslin as the moon shines clearly in green water, and the jewels blazed like stars with red and blue fires at each movement of their limbs. Their heads were crowned simply with white clematis, and the glory of their straight-featured Circassian faces, together with the unrivalled contours of softly moulded throat and breast and perfect limbs, veiled only so much as a light mist may veil, would have taken the breath away of the most inveterate frequenter of the Alhambra and Empire in dull old England. Hamilton drew in his breath with a little start as he first saw the semicircle, but it was not on the Circassians that his eyes were fixed, but on the very centre figure of that beautiful half-moon. Set in the centre, she seemed to be considered the pearl amongst them, as indeed she was. The mist that enveloped her was not pale green as the veils of the other two, but white, and the beautiful perfect form that it enclosed was of a warmer, brighter tint than theirs.

The white films of the drapery fell from the base of her throat, leaving her arms quite bare, but softly clinging to breast and flanks, till a gold band resting on her hips confined it closely, and depressed in the centre, was fastened by a single enormous ruby, the one spot of blood-red colour upon her. Beneath the sloping belt of gold fell her loose Turkish trousers of gleaming white, transparent tissue, clasped at the ankles by bands of gold. On her feet were little Turkish slippers, on her brow - nothing, but the crown of her radiant youth and beauty. Hamilton, gazing at it across the footlights, thought he had never seen, either pictured or in the flesh, a face so beautiful, so full of the beauty, the goodness, the power and wonder of life.

The sight thrilled him. Like the power of electricity, its power began to run along his veins, heating them, stirring them, calling upon nerve and muscle and sense to wake up. He looked, and life itself seemed to stream into him through his eyes. The girl's face was a well-rounded oval, supported on the round, perfect column of her throat; the eyes seemed pools of blackness that had caught all the splendour and the radiance of a thousand Eastern nights. The fires of many stars, the whole brilliance of the purple nights of Asia were mirrored in them. Above them rose the dark, arching span of the eyebrows on the soft warm-tinted forehead, cut in one line of severest beauty with the delicate nose. Beneath, the curling lips were like the flowers of the pomegranate, a living, vivid scarlet, and the rounded chin had the contour and bloom of the nectarine.

She smiled faintly as she met the fixed gaze of Hamilton's eyes across the footlights - such an innocent, merry little smile it seemed, not the mechanical contortions one buys with pieces of silver. Hamilton's blood seemed to catch light at it and flame all over his body. He sat upright in his seat: gone were his fatigue, his thirst, his eye-ache. His frame felt no more discomfort: his whole soul rushed to his eyes, and sat there watching. In some men their physical constitution is so closely knitted to the mental, that the slightest shock to either instantly vibrates through the other and works its effect equally on both. Hamilton was of this order, and his body responded, instantly now, to the joy and interest born suddenly in his mind.

A moment after the curtain was rolled up, a huge negro, dressed in a fancy dress of scarlet, and with a high cap of the same colour on his head, came on from the side. In his hand he carried a small dog-whip, and as he cracked it all the girls stood up. Hamilton sickened as he looked at him: an indefinable feeling of horror came over him as this man stalked about the stage. He pointed with his whip to the two African girls at the end of the semicircle, and they came forward, while the rest sat down. A horrid uneasy feeling of discomfort grew up in Hamilton, similar to that which a lover of animals feels, when called upon to witness performing dogs, and all the fear and anxiety pent up in their fast-beating little hearts is communicated to himself. He watched the girls' faces keenly as the negro went round and placed himself behind the middle chair of the semicircle, while the two Africans danced. Hamilton hardly noticed their dance, a curious barbaric performance that would have been alarming to the British matron, but was neither new nor interesting to Hamilton. He kept his eyes fixed on the white-clothed girl in the centre, and the sinister figure behind her chair. She seemed calm and indifferent, and when the negro put his hand on her shoulder looked up and listened to his words without fear or repulsion. Hamilton, keenly alive, with every sense alert, sat in his chair, a prey to the new and delightful feeling, not known for years, of interest.

Yes, he was interested, and the energetic sense of loathing for the negro proved it. The music, loud and strident - an ordinary Italian piano-organ having been introduced amongst the Oriental instruments - banged on, and then abruptly came to a stop when the negro cracked his whip. The two African women resumed their chairs, there was some applause, and a good many small coins fell on the stage from the hands of the audience. The second pair of girls rose, came forward and commenced to dance, the organ playing some appropriate Spanish airs. After these, the two Indian girls who gave the usual *dance de ventre* to a lively Italian air on the organ. Then, at last, *she* rose from her chair and approached the footlights. The organ ceased playing, only the Indian music continued: wild sensual music, imitating at intervals the cries of passion.

To this accompaniment the girl danced.

Had any British matrons been present we must hope they would have walked out, yet, to the eye of the artist, there was nothing coarse or offending, simply a most beautiful harmony of motion. The girl's beauty, her grace and youth, and the slight lissomness of all her body lent to the dance a poetry, a refinement it would not have possessed with another exponent.

Moreover, though there was a certain ardour in her looks and gestures, in the way she yielded her limbs and body to the influence of the music, yet there was also a gay innocence, a bright naive irresponsibility in it that contrasted strongly with the sinister intention underlying all the movements of the other two Indian dancers. At the end of the dance Hamilton took a rupee from his pocket and threw it across the tin lamps towards her feet. She picked it up smiling, though she left the other coins which fell on the stage untouched, and went back to her chair.

After her dance, the great negro came forward and did a turn of his own. Hamilton looked away. What was this man to the little circle? he wondered. He could not keep his mind off that one query? Were they his slaves? willing or unwilling? did they constitute his harem? or were they paid, independent workers? His mind was made up to get speech with this one girl, at least, that evening. This delightful feeling of interest, this pleasure, even this keen disgust, all were so welcome to him in the dreary mental state of indifference that had become his habit, that he welcomed them eagerly, and could not let them go. Beyond this there was rising within him, suddenly and overwhelmingly, the force of Life, indignant at the long repression it had been subjected to. Man may be a civilized being, accustomed to the artificial restraints and laws he has laid upon himself, but there remains within him still that primitive nature that knows nothing, and never will learn anything of those laws, and which leaps up suddenly after years of its prison-life in overpowering revolt, and says, "Joy is my birthright. I will have it!"

This moment is the crisis of most lives. It was with Hamilton now, and it seemed suddenly to him that twenty years of fidelity to an unloved, unloving woman was enough. The debt contracted at the altar twenty years before had been paid off. The promise, given under a misunderstanding to one who had wilfully deceived him, was wiped out. It was a marvel to him in those moments how it had held him so long.

Hamilton had one of those keen, brilliant minds that make their decisions quickly, and rarely regret them. He took his resolution now. That prisoner in revolt within him should be free; he would strike off the fetters he had worn too long and vainly. He was before the open book of Life, at that page where he had stood so long. With a firm decisive hand he would take the new page, and turn it over. That last page, on which his wife's name was written large, was completely done with, closed.

The old joyous spirit, the keen eagerness for love and joy and life, the Pagan's gay rejoicing in it, that had been such a marked feature of his disposition before his marriage, came back to him, rushed through him, refilled him.

His marriage, with its disillusionment, had crushed it out of him for a time, and, with that same decisiveness that marked him now, he had turned over the pages of youthful dreams and joys and loves, and opened the next page of work, of strenuous endeavour, of a hard, rigid observance of fidelity to the vows he had taken. And for a time work and its rewards, effort and its returns, a hard, practical life in the world amongst men, had held him. That now was no longer to be all to him.

His life, and such joy as it might hold for him, was to be his own again. The joy of the decisions filled him, elated him. He felt as if his mind had sudden wings, and could lift him with it to the roof.

Such a decision, when it comes, seems to oneself, as it seemed to Hamilton now, a sudden thing. It has the force and shock of a revelation, but it is not really sudden. The great rebellion nearly all natures - certainly some, and these usually the greatest and best - feel at the absence of joy in their lives had been gradually growing within him, gathering a little strength each day. It is only the climax of such feelings that is sudden - the awakening of the mind to their presence. The growth has been going on day by day, week by week, unmeasured, unreckoned with.

Immediately the curtain fell, Hamilton left his seat and went up to a door, reached by a few steps, on the level of the footlights, and at the left side of them. No one hindered him. The rest of the audience were going out. He pushed the door, which yielded readily, and he passed through. A narrow, white-washed, lath-and-plaster passage opened before him, at the end of which he saw a tin lamp burning against the wall and heard voices.

The passage led into a three-cornered room, where he found some of the dancers and an old woman who was huddled up on a straw mat in the corner. The negro was not there. The girls stood about idly; some were changing their clothes. They did not seem to heed his presence, except the one he was seeking, who came straight towards him. As she moved across the dirty, littered room, her limbs under their transparent covering moved, and her head was carried with the air of an empress. "Will the Sahib come with me?" she said in a low, soft tone. She raised her eyes to his face. They were wide, enquiring, like the deer's brought face to face with the hunter in the green thickets.

The other girls glanced towards him, and some smiles were exchanged, but no one approached him. They seemed to understand he was there only for the star of the troupe. Hamilton looked down into those glorious midnight eyes fixed upon him, and a faint colour came into his cheek.

"I will come wherever you lead," he answered in Hindustani. These surroundings were horrible, but the shade of them did not seem to dim her charm.

The scent in the air was disagreeable. Tawdry spangles and false jewels lay about on the tumble-down settees. From behind little doors that opened from the walls round came the sound of men's voices.

"Let the Sahib come this way, then," she answered, and turned towards one of the small doors in the wall. This took them into another tiny, musty-smelling passage that wound about like the run of a rabbit warren, only wide enough for one to pass along at a time, and the strips of lath were so low overhead that Hamilton bent his neck involuntarily to avoid them.

At a door in the side of this she stopped and pushed it open; the little run way wound on beyond in the darkness.

Hamilton followed her into the sloping-roofed, lath-and-plaster pent-house that had been run up between the back of the stage and the wall of the building. Native lamps were hooked into the wall, and their light showed the garish ugliness of it all - the hastily whitewashed walls, the scraps of ragged, dirty, scarlet cloth hung here and there over a bulge or stain in the plaster: the boarded floor, uneven and cracked: the bed against the wall, not too clean looking, its dingy curtains not quite concealing the dingier pillows; the broken chair on which a basin stood, placed on two grey-looking towels; another chair with the back rails knocked out leaning against the wall.

He threw his gaze round it in a moment's rapid survey, then he pressed to the rickety, uneven door and shot the bolt.

The girl stood in the middle of the room, an exquisitely lovely figure. She regarded him with wide, innocent eyes. Hamilton felt all the blood alight in his veins; it seemed to him he could hear his pulses beating. Never in his life before had joy and passion met within him to stir him as they did now, but in natures where there is a strong, deep strain of intellectuality the body never quite conquers the mind, the light of the intellect never quite goes down, however strong the sea, however high the waves of animal passion on which it rides; and now Hamilton felt the great appeal to his brain as well as to his senses that the girl's beauty made.

He went up to her. She looked at him with an intense admiration, almost worship in her eyes. A man at such moments looks, as Nature intended he should, his very best, and Hamilton's face, of a noble and splendid type, lighted now by the keenest animation, held her gaze.

"Tell me," he said in a low tone, for footsteps passed on the creaking boards, and gibbering voices and laughter could be heard outside, "tell me, what is that man to you? Do you belong to him, all of you?"

"That...? He is not a man, he is a ... nothing," replied the girl, looking up with calm, glorious eyes. "He can do no harm ... nor good."

Hamilton drew a quick breath.

"You dance like this every evening, and then choose someone in the audience in this way?" he questioned, slipping his hand round her neck and looking down at her, a half-amused sadness coming into his eyes.

The girl shook her head with a quick negation.

"No, I have only been here a few days - a week, I think. Did you notice that old woman as we came through here? I belong to her; she taught me to dance. She brought me here, and I dance for the Nothing, but I have never taken any one like this before. The other girls do, every night, but each night the Nothing said to me, 'No one here to-night, good enough. Wait till an English Sahib comes.'"

Hamilton listened with a paling cheek; his breath came and went faintly; he hardly seemed to draw it; he put his next question very gently, watching her open brow and proud, fearless eyes.

"Do you know nothing of men at all, then?"

"Nothing, Sahib, nothing," she answered, falling on her knees suddenly at his feet, and raising her hands towards him. "This will be my bridal night with the Sahib. The Nothing told me to please you, to do all you told me. What shall I do? how shall I please you?"

Hamilton looked down upon her: his brain seemed whirling; the pulses along his veins beat heavily; new worlds, new vistas of life seemed opening before him as he looked at her, so beautiful in her first youth, in her unclouded innocence, full, it is true, of Oriental passion, with a certain Oriental absence of shame, but untouched, able to be his, and his only.

Before he could speak again, or collect his thoughts that the girl's words had scattered, her soft voice went on:

"Surely the Sahib is a god, not a man. I have seen the men across the footlights: there were none like the Sahib. I said to my mother, 'I do not like men, I do not want them; what shall I do?' And my mother said, 'There is no hurry, my child; we will wait till a rich Sahib comes.' But you are not a man, you must be a god, you are so beautiful; and I am the slave of the Sahib, for ever and ever."

She looked up at him, great lights seemed to have been lighted in the midnight pools of her eyes, the curved lips parted a little, showing the perfect, even teeth; the rounded, warm-hued cheeks glowed; the lids of her eyes lifted as those of a person looking out into a new world.

Hamilton stood looking at her, and two great seas of conflicting emotions swept into his brain, and under their tumult he remained irresolute. Mere instincts and nature, the common impulse of the male to take his pleasure whenever offered, prompted him to draw her to his breast and let her learn the great joy of life in his arms; but some higher feeling held him back: the knowledge that the first way in which a woman learns these things colours her whole after estimation of them, restrained him.

Here he saw, suddenly, there was new ground for Love to build himself a habitation upon. Should it be but a rude shanty, loosely constructed of Desire? Was it not rather such a fair and lovely site that it was worthy a perfect temple, built and finished with delicate care?

This flower of wonderful bloom he had found by chance in such a poor, rough garden, was it not better to carry it gently to some sheltered spot, to transplant and keep it for his own, rather than just tear at it with a careless touch in passing by?

Hamilton had the brain of the artist and the poet; things touched him less by their reality than by that strange halo imagination throws round them.

The sound of some shuffling steps in the passage outside, a lurch as of some drunken and unsteady figure, some whispered words, and then a burst of ribald laughter just outside the door, decided him. No: her wedding night should not be here. Keen in his sympathy with women, Hamilton knew how often that night recurs to a woman's thoughts, and should its memories always bring back to her this loathsome shed, these hideous sounds?

A repulsion so great filled him that it swept back his desire for the moment. A great eagerness to get her away unharmed, unsoiled from such a place, filled him. Already she seemed to be part of himself, to be a possession he must guard. His heart was empty and hungry: by means of her beauty and this strange unexpected innocence she had so suddenly revealed to him, she had leapt into it, made it her own. He sat down on the mean, dingy bed, and drew her warm, supple body into his arms: she stood within their circle submissively, quivering with pleasure. His touch was very gentle and reverent, for he was a man who knew the value of essentials; his brain was keen enough to go down to them and judge of them, undeterred and unhindered and undeceived by externals, by fictitious emblems. He saw here that he was in the presence of a tender, youthful, unformed mind of complete innocence, and the abhorrent surroundings affected that essential not at all.

A married woman in his own rank, with her dozen lovers and her knowledge of evil, high in the favour of the world, could never have had from him the same reverence that he gave to this dancing-girl of the Deccan, who in the world's eyes was but a creature put under his feet for him to trample on.

"Would you like to leave all these people and come to live only with me? dance only for me?" he said softly, looking into those great wondering eyes fixed in awe upon his face.

"Would you like to have a house to yourself, and a garden full of flowers, and stay there with me alone?"

The girl clasped her hands joyously, smile after smile rippled over the brilliant face.

"Oh, Sahib, it would be paradise! If I can stay with the Sahib, I shall be happy anywhere. I am the slave of the Sahib. If he but use me as the mat before his door to walk upon, I shall be content."

Hamilton shivered. He drew her a little closer. "Hush! I do not like to hear you say those things. You shall come to me and sleep in my arms, but not to-night. Love is a very great thing: it will be a great thing with us, and it must not be thought of lightly, do you see? Will you stay here and think of me only till I come again? Think of your bridal night with me, dream of me till I come back for you?"

"The Sahib's will is my law; but even if I wished, I could think of nothing else but him till I see him again," she responded, her eyes fixed upon his face. Hamilton gazed upon her. She made such a lovely picture standing there: he thought he had never seen beauty so perfect, so exquisitely fresh. The soft transparent tunic did not conceal it, only lightly veiled its bloom. Her breasts, rounded and firm, stood out as a statue's. They seemed to express the vigour of her buoyant youth: they had never known artificial support, and needed none. The waist was naturally slight, the hips also, the straight supple limbs and round arms were the most richly-modelled parts, perhaps, of the whole perfect form.

Hamilton slipped his arm down to her yielding waist and drew her closer. Then he bent his head and kissed the wonderfully-carved and glowing mouth. With a little cry of joy the girl threw both arms about his neck and kissed him back with a wealth of fervour in her lips, pressing her soft bosom against his in all the natural, unrestrained ardour of a first and new-found love.

"Sahib, Sahib! do not leave me long. Come and take me away soon! I am all yours! No other shall see me till you come again."

Hamilton was satisfied. He raised his head, his whole ardent nature aflame.

"Dear little girl, let us go then to the old woman, and perhaps I can pay her enough to make her take you away from here, and keep you safe till I can come for you."

"Come, Sahib, come!" she answered, joyfully drawing out of his arms and running across the room; she unbolted the door and pulled it open, nearly causing the old woman who was crouched just outside, and apparently leaning against it, to roll into the room.

"Saidie, Saidie! you have no respect for me," she grumbled, getting on her feet with some difficulty. Hamilton came up, and helped to balance her as she stood.

"Your Saidie pleases me very much," he said, drawing out a pocket-book. "I want to take her away from here altogether. How much do you ask for her?"

The old woman's beady-black eyes twinkled and gleamed, and fixed on the pocket-book.

"It is not possible, Sahib," she said in a grumbling tone, "for me to part with her and her services. A girl like that with her beauty, her dancing, her singing! She will earn gold every night. Let the Sahib come here each evening if he will and take his turn with the rest. For a girl like that to go to one man alone is waste and folly."

The colour mounted to Hamilton's face. His brows contracted.

"What I have to say is this," he answered sternly and briefly, "I want this girl, and if you take her with you to some place of safety for to-night, I will come to-morrow or the next day and give you 2000 rupees for her - no more and no less. I have spoken."

"Two thousand rupees!" replied shrilly the old woman, "for Saidie, the star of the dancers, and not yet fifteen! No, Sahib, no! a Parsee will give more than that for a half hour with her."

Hamilton caught the old creature by her skinny arm:

"You waste your words talking to me," he said. "I am a police magistrate, and I can have your whole place here closed, and all of you put in prison, if I choose. The girl is willing to come with me, and I will take her and pay you well for her. You have her ready for me to-morrow night, or you go to prison - which you please." The old woman shivered at the word magistrate, and fell trembling on her knees.

"Let the Sahib have mercy! That great black brute will kill me if the police come here. I take Saidie to my house, the Sahib comes there when he will. He pays, he has her. It is all finished."

She spread out her thin black hands in a shaking gesture of finality, and then fell forward and kissed Hamilton's boots after the complimentary but embarrassing manner of natives. Hamilton drew back a little. He was angered that Saidie should be witness, auditor of all this. She stood silent, passive, gazing at the hot, angry colour mounting to his face. He bent forward and dragged the old woman up by her arms.

"Take this for yourself now," he said, putting a hundred-rupee note into her hand, "and make no more difficulty. Take every care of Saidie, and you will have your two thousand rupees very shortly."

The old woman seized the note, and began to mumble blessings on Hamilton, which he cut short: "Give me the name of your street and the house where you live, that I may find you easily," he said, and noted down the directions she gave him. Then he turned to the girl and put his arm round her neck.

"Dear Saidie! I trust to you. Remember it is your innocence, your virtue, I love more than your beauty. Do not dance nor let anyone see you till I come again."

He kissed her on the lips as she promised him. The soft, warm form thrilled against him as their lips met. Then with a mental wrench he turned and went out of the room and quickly down the dark passage.

At the end his way was barred by the immense form of the negro.

"Something for me, master; do not forget me! I keep the pretty things here for the gentlemen to see."

Hamilton drew back with loathing. Then he reflected - it was better, perhaps, to keep all smooth.

He dived into his pockets and found a roll of small notes, which he pushed into the negro's hand. The man bowed and let him pass, and Hamilton went on out into the street.

It was evening now. The calm, lovely golden light of an Indian evening fell all around him as he walked rapidly back to his bungalow. As he entered it, how different he felt from the man who had left it that morning! How light his footstep, how bright and keen the tone of his voice! It quite surprised himself as he called out to his butler that he was ready for dinner. Then he bounded up to his room humming. His very muscles were of quite a different texture seemingly now from an hour or two ago! How the blood flew about joyously in his body! Dear Venus! she makes us pay generally, but who can cavil at the glorious gifts she gives? As soon as his dinner was disposed of, and all his other servants had retired from the room, Hamilton called his butler, Pir Bakhs, to him, and held a long conference with that intelligent and trustworthy individual. Hamilton was one of those men that by reason of his strikingly good looks, his charm of manner, his consideration for others, and his complete control over himself that never allowed him to be betrayed into an unjust word or action was greatly liked by every one, and simply worshipped by his servants and all those in any way in a position dependent on him.

When to-night Pir Bakhs was honoured by his confidence, the servant's whole will and all his keen energies rose with delight to serve his master. After he had listened in silence to Hamilton's wishes, he proceeded to make himself master of the whole scheme, detail by detail.

"The Sahib wishes a very beautiful bungalow far out, away from the city? I know of one house across the desert; my cousin was butler there. The Sahib went away to England, and the bungalow is to be let furnished. Have I the Sahib's permission to go down to bazaar, see my cousin to-night? I make all arrangements. I go to-morrow morning; I get cook and all other servants. I stay there and make all ready for the Sahib to-morrow evening."

Hamilton smiled at the man's eagerness to serve him. He knew well that secretly in his heart his Mahommedan butler had always deplored the severely monastic style in which he had lived, the absence of women in his master's bungalow, the emptiness of his arms that should have had to bear his master's children, and that he now was ready to welcome heartily his master's reformation.

"Could you really do all that, Pir Bakhs?" he asked; "and can you assure me that the house is a good one, and has the compound been well kept up?"

"The house is about the same as this, but not quite so large. It is in the oasis of Deira, across the desert. The Sahib knows how well the palms grow there. My cousin tells me the compound is very large; the Sahib there kept four malis;[1] very fine garden, many English roses there."

[Footnote 1: Gardeners.]

"English roses I do not care for, Pir Bakhs," returned Hamilton with a melancholy smile. "The roses of the East are far fairer to me."

The butler bowed with his hand to his forehead. He took his master's speech as a gracious compliment to his country.

"Everything grow there," he answered, spreading out his hands: "pomegranates, bamboo, mangoes, bananas, sago palm, cocoanut palm, magnolia - everything. I go to-morrow, I engage malis; I have all ready for the Sahib."

"Very well, I trust you with it all. I shall keep on this house just as it is, and leave most of the servants here. You and your wives must come out with me, and you engage any other necessary servants and hire any extra furniture you want."

"The Sahib is very good to his servant," returned the butler, his face lighting up joyfully. "When will the Sahib shed the light of his countenance on the bungalow?"

"I will try to run out to see it, to-morrow, after office hours," replied Hamilton, "if you will have all ready by then. I shall look over it, and return to dine here as usual. Then about ten or later, I will come over and bring your new mistress out with me. You must have a good supper waiting for us. Take over all the linen and plate you may want, but see that enough is left in this house so that I can entertain the English Sahibs here if I want to, and let my riding camel be well fed early. I shall use him for coming and going. That's all, I think."

The butler bowed, and retired radiant with joyous importance, and Hamilton sat on alone by the table thinking. The blood ran at high tide along his veins, his eyes glowed, looking into space. Life, he thought, what a joyous thing it was when it stretched out its hands full of gifts!

CHAPTER II

The following afternoon, directly his work at the office was finished, he went out to the oasis in the desert to look at his new possession, his bungalow in the palms.

The moment he saw it peeping out from amongst them, and surrounded by roses, he expressed himself satisfied, and named the place Saied-i-stan, or the place of happiness.

The butler met him there; he was bursting with self-importance.

"You leave everything to me, Sahib - everything. I know all the Sahib wants. He shall have all. Let him come, ten o'clock, nine o'clock, no matter when; all quite ready. I am here. I have everything waiting for the Sahib."

Hamilton smiled and praised him, and went back to the station; took a pretence of dinner and a hurried cup of coffee, and then went down into the bazaar with the precious bit of paper containing the directions to Saidie's dwelling-place in his breast pocket.

He found the house at last, and, going in at the doorless entrance, climbed patiently the wooden stairs that ran straight up from it in complete darkness. On the topmost landing - a frail wooden structure that creaked beneath his feet - he paused, and rapped twice on the door opposite him.

Victoria Cross

His heart beat rapidly as he stood there; the blood seemed flying through it. All the strength of his vigorous body seemed gathering itself together within him, all the fire of his keen, hungry brain leapt up, and waiting there in the dark on the narrow landing he knew the joy of life.

The door was opened. In a moment his eye swept round the interior of the high windowless room. The floor was bare, with mats here and there, and in the centre stood a flat pan of charcoal, glowing under a closed and steaming cooking-pot. At one end a coarse chick, suspended from a wooden bar, dropped its long lines to the floor, and behind this, on some cushions, sat Saidie with another of the dancing-girls.

The old woman who had opened the door, salaamed, touching the floor with her forehead as Hamilton walked in, and then securely shut and fastened the door behind him. Saidie rose and looked through the shimmering lines of the chick at him as he entered.

Very handsome the tall commanding figure looked in the mean, bare room: the long neck and well-modelled head, with its black, close-cut hair, stood out a noble relief against the colourless wall, and the clear brown skin, with the warm tint of quick blood in it that showed above the English collar, arrested the girl's eyes with a keen thrill of joy. Looking at him, she felt rushing through her the passionate delight that self-surrender to such a man would be. Without waiting to be summoned, she parted the lines of the chick, came out from them, and fell on her knees at his feet.

The heat in the shut-up room was very great, and she was wearing only a straight white muslin tunic, through which all the soft beauty of her form could be seen, as an English face is seen through a veil. Her hair was looped back from her brows and tied simply with a piece of green ribbon, as an English girl's might have been, and flowed in its thick, black glossy waves to her waist.

Hamilton bent over her and raised her in his arms, feeling in that moment, though the whole universe were reeling and rocking round him to its ruin, he would care nothing while he pressed that soft breast to his.

The old woman sat down cross-legged by the charcoal, and began to fan it.

The other girl behind the chick looked out curiously, but her eyes never noted the strength and beauty of Hamilton's figure, nor the bright glow in the oval cheek: she looked to see if he wore rings on his fingers, and tried to catch sight of the links in his cuffs to see if they were silver or gold.

Saidie had the divine gift of passion: all the fire of the gods in her veins. Zenobie had none, and Saidie's joy now was something she could not understand.

"Have you come to take me away, now at once?" Saidie murmured in a soft, passionate whisper close to his ear, and the accent of joy and delight went quivering down through the deepest recesses of the man's being.

"Yes: are you ready to come with me?" Needless question! put only for the supreme pleasure of listening to its answer.

"Oh, more than ready," whispered the soft voice back. "How shall the slave explain her longing to her lord?"

Zenobie had come round the chick, while they stood by the door, and drawn forward the one little low wooden stool that they possessed. She came up now, and pulled at Saidie's sleeve.

"Let the Sahib be seated," she said reprovingly, and Saidie let her arms slip from his neck and drew him forward to the stool by the charcoal pan.

With some difficulty Hamilton drew up his long legs and seated himself cautiously on the small seat; Saidie and Zenobie sat cross-legged on the ground close to his feet. The old woman ceased to fan the fire; the bright red glow of the coals fell softly on the strong, noble beauty of the man's face, and Saidie, looking up to it, sat speechless, her bosom heaving, her lips parted, her dark eyes full of mysterious fires, melting, swimming, behind their veil of lashes.

Zenobie watched her with curiosity: what did she feel for this infidel who wore no rings and only silver in his cuffs?

Hamilton, as soon as he was seated, drew out his pocket-book - old and worn, for he spent little on himself - and opened it.

The old woman sat up. Zenobie's eyes gleamed: the business was going to commence. Only Saidie did not stir nor move her eyes from his face.

"Two thousand rupees was the price agreed upon; here it is," he said, taking out a thick bundle of notes that occupied the whole inside of the poor, limp pocket-book; and as the old woman stretched out a skinny claw for them and began to slowly count them, he turned his gaze away, on to the upturned face of the girl watching him with sensual adoration.

The old woman counted through the notes, and then securely tied them into the end of her chudda.

"The sum is the due sum, well counted," she said, looking up; "and when will my lord take his slave?"

"To-night," Hamilton replied briefly, but not without a swift enquiring glance into the girl's eyes. Though he had bought and paid for her, he could not get out of the Western knack of considering that the girl's desires had to be consulted.

The old woman raised her hands in affected horror.

"To-night! But she is not well clothed, she is not bathed and anointed; the bridal robes are not prepared. My lord, it cannot be!"

Hamilton looked at Saidie; she crept to his side and put her head on his breast.

"Yes, to-night, take me to-night," she murmured eagerly; he smiled, and put his arm around her.

"The bridal clothes are of no consequence," he answered decisively. "My camel waits below. I will take her to-night."

"She has no shoes," objected the old woman. "She cannot descend the stairs."

"I will carry her down," replied Hamilton, and, springing up from the little stool, he stooped over the lovely form at his feet, raising her into his arms, close to his breast. Saidie clung to his neck with a little cry of pleasure, her bare, warm-tinted feet hung over his arm.

The old woman gasped: Zenobie laughed. The Englishman looked so big, so immensely strong. The weight of Saidie, tall and well-developed as she was, seemed as nothing to him.

"Zenobie, will you hold the lamp at the doorway, that he may see his way?" Saidie cried out, slipping off a thin gold circlet she wore on her arm, and letting it drop into the other's hands.

"Farewell, Zenobie; may you be always as happy as I am now."

Zenobie caught the bracelet and ran to the wall, unhooked the lamp that hung there, and came to the door.

"Farewell, my mother," Saidie said, as they turned to it.

"Farewell, my daughter; be submissive to the Sahib, and obey him in all things."

The door was opened, and by the dim, uncertain light of

Zenobie's lamp, Hamilton, clasping his warm, living burden, went slowly and heavily down the bending stairs, feeling the life brimming in every vein.

Outside, in the tranquil splendour of the starry Eastern night, knelt the camel, peacefully awaiting its lord, and as Hamilton approached it with his burden, it turned its head and large, liquid eyes upon him with a gurgle of pleasure.

"The camel loves Hamilton Sahib," murmured the girl, as he set her on the soft red cloth laid over the animal's back, which formed the only saddle. He took his own place in front of her.

"Hold to my belt firmly," he told her, gathering into his hand the light rein. "Are you ready for him to rise?"

He felt her little, soft hands glide in between his belt and waist.

"Yes, I am quite ready," she answered, and at a word of encouragement, the great beast rose with its slow, stately swing to its feet, and Hamilton guided it towards the Meidan. The soft, hot air stirred against their faces as they moved through the night.

Nothing could present a more lovely picture than the bungalow that evening. A low, white house, looking in the moonlight as if built of marble, surrounded by masses of palms which threw a delicate tracery of shadow upon it and drooped their beautiful, fan-like, feathery branches over it, between it and the jewelled sky.

A light verandah ran around the lower of the two stories, completely covered by the white, star-like bloom of the jessamine that poured forth floods of fragrance like incense on the hot, still air, and a giant pink magnolia rioted over the wide porch of lattice-work. Within it was brightly lighted, and a warm glow from shaded lamps came out from each window, stealing softly through the veil of scented jessamine and falling on the masses of pink roses surrounding the house.

The deep peace, the sweet scent in the silence, the kiss of the moonlight and the starlight on the sleeping flowers, the exquisite form of the shadows on the white wall, filled Hamilton with pleasure: each sense seemed subtly ministered to; he felt as if invisible spirits round him were feeding him with ambrosia.

He turned round to Saidie as the camel slowly and majestically entered the compound gate, and saw her clearly framed in the soft silver light; all this wondrous beauty round them seemed to be to her beauty but as the harmonies that in an opera float round the central air. And she smiled as he turned upon her.

"How do you like your new house, Saidie?" he said, half laughing as he leant back to her.

"Surely it is Paradise, Sahib," she murmured back in awestruck tones.

Within the door waited the servants to welcome them in a double line, and as Saidie entered, they fell flat with their faces on the floor. She passed through the prostrate row saluting them, and on to the foot of the stairs. The ayah that the butler had engaged rose and followed her mistress upstairs, where she was ushered into her bath and dressing-room; while the butler, swelling with importance and joyous pride, led Hamilton to the large room he had prepared as a bedroom on the first floor. As they went in Hamilton gave a murmur of approval very dear to the man's heart, as he heard it, standing respectfully by the door.

The room was large, and two windows, draped with curtains, stood open to the soft night.

The bed in the centre of the room was one of the wide Indian charpais which are unrivalled for comfort, and glimmered softly white beneath its filmy mosquito curtains in the lamplight shed by four handsome rose-shaded lamps. Small tables stood everywhere, bearing vases of fresh flowers, roses, and stephanotis; a rich, deep rose-coloured carpet spread all over the floor, with only a small border of chetai visible round the walls; and two easy-chairs of the same colour and numerous smaller ones piled up with cushions completed the equipment of the room. The air was full of scent, and the scheme of colour in the room perfect. Nothing but rose and white was allowed to meet the eye. The flowers were selected with this view, and the great bowls of roses all blushed the same glorious tint through the snowy whiteness of the stephanotis.

The room suggested, in its softly-lighted glow of pink and white, a bridal chamber.

Hamilton turned to his servant with a pleased smile on his handsome, animated face.

"You are an artist, Pir Bakhs, and a sort of magician, to do all this in twelve hours."

Pir Bakhs bowed and salaamed by the door, his well-formed polished face wreathed in many smiles.

Downstairs the girl was already waiting for her lord, bathed, and with her long hair shaken out and brushed after the dust of the desert ride, and looped back from her forehead by a fresh green ribbon. She did not sit down, but stood waiting.

This room showed the same care as the upper one, and the table was laid out with Hamilton's plate and glass and four beautiful epergnes held the flowers.

Natives are artists, particularly in colour arrangements; the whole colour scheme here was white and green, and any table in Belgravia would have had hard work to equal this one. Saidie stood looking at it, and the servants, already ranged by the sideboard, stood with their eyes on the ground, yet conscious of her wonderful beauty, and pleased by it in the same way that they would have felt pride and pleasure in the beauty and good condition of a new horse or camel acquired by their master.

After a few minutes Hamilton came down. He had put on his evening clothes as they had been laid out for him by the bearer, and looked radiant as he entered.

Saidie gave a little cry as she saw him. His present dress, well cut and close-fitting, showed his splendid figure to greater advantage than the loose suit she had seen him in hitherto. His long neck carried his fine, spirited head erect, and the masses of thick, black hair, with just the least wave in it, shone in the lamplight. His well-cut face, with its gay animation and charming, debonair, unaffected expression, made a kingly and perfect picture to the girl's dazzled eyes.

As they took their places and their soup was served, she could not detach her gaze from his face.

He laughed as he looked at her.

"Come, you must be hungry. Take your soup while it's hot; don't waste your time looking at me."

"Sahib, I cannot help looking at you. You are so wonderful to me! Please give me leave to. I do not want any soup."

Hamilton, who by this time had finished his own, leant back in his chair and laughed again, looking at her with eyes blazing with mirth and passion. This innocent, genuine admiration was very pleasing to him in its flattery; this worship offered to himself, rather than his gifts, was something new to him, and the girl's beauty sent all the fires of life in quick streams through his frame as he looked on it. He was alive for the first time in his existence, and filled with a surprised happiness as great as the girl's. He was as virgin to joy as she was to love. "You are the dearest little girl I ever knew," he said; "but if you won't take soup, you must eat fish. Yes, I positively refuse you my permission to look at me till you have finished that whole plate."

Saidie dropped her eyes to her fish very submissively at this, while Hamilton himself filled her glass.

"Have you ever tasted wine?" he asked. "This is champagne; drink it, and tell me what you think of it."

"All my people are Mahommedans; we do not drink wine," Saidie replied, taking up the glass and sipping from it.

"Perhaps you won't like it," he suggested, watching her.

"If the Sahib gives it to me I shall like it," replied Saidie, smiling at him over the delicate golden glass: it threw its light upwards into her great gleaming eyes, and Hamilton kissed the little hand that put the glass gently down on the table again.

Next after the fish came game and joints, course after course, more food in that one meal than Saidie was accustomed to see for many people for a week. Her own appetite was soon satisfied, and she sat for the most part gazing at Hamilton, with her hands tightly locked together in her lap: such a nervous delight filled her, such a strange joy in knowing herself to be alive, to be possessed of a beautiful body that by reason of its beauty was worthy the caresses of a man like this; such a pure rapture animated every fibre, to realise that it was in her power to give pleasure to him. With such feelings as these no faintest hint of humiliation or degradation could mingle. Saidie felt only that superb and joyous pride that Nature originally intended the female to have in her surrender to the male.

Her very breath seemed to flutter softly with joyous trepidation and excitement as it passed over her lips. That she was to be his, held in his arms, admitted to his embrace, seemed to her to be the crown of her life, an honour given by special divine favour.

So must Rhea Sylvia have felt praying before her Vestal altar when Mars first appeared to her startled eyes.

And Hamilton, with his keen, sensitive temperament, saw into her mind clearly, and was fully aware of all this fervent adoration, this intense passionate worship springing within her; and an immense tenderness and reverence grew up within him, enclosing all his passion as the crystal vessel encloses the crimson wine.

That she would not in her present state have shrunk or flinched from a knife, if only his hand held it while it wounded her, he knew quite well, and this wonderful voluntary self-sacrifice which is the soul of all female passion appealed to him as a very holy thing.

He knew that constantly this adoring love was poured out by women for men, that almost every virgin heart beats with this same worship as the first pain of love enters it, but ah! for how short a time! How quickly the man tears open those eyes that would so willingly be closed to his vileness! how soon come the infidelity, the lies and the meanness, the trickery and the treachery! How assiduously the man teaches the woman who loves him that there is nothing in him worthy of adoration, not even admiration, not even decent respect! How little confidence, how little credence she soon gives to his word that was once so sacred to her! How in her heart, though her lips say nothing, is that once rapturous worship changed into a measureless contempt!

Men persistently teach women that they must not expect the best from them, but the lowest. And the women cry in pain as they see the white mantle of their love trampled upon and dragged in the mire of lies and falseness, and they take it back from the base hands and burn it in the fires kindled in their outraged hearts. Something of this flashed through Hamilton's brain as he met the adoring trust and love in the girl's eyes, and an unspoken vow formed itself within him that he would not deceive and betray it, that his lips should not lie to her, that to the end he would be to her as she now saw him in the glamour of those first hours.

When he had tempted her to every sweet and bon-bon on the table, and made her drink all the wine he thought good for her, he sent the servants away, and they remained alone together in the dining-room with their coffee before them. He put his arm round her, and drawing her out of her own chair, took her on to his knees and pressed her head down on his shoulder.

"Are you not tired with that long ride on the camel?" he asked.

"No, Sahib, I am not tired."

The soft weight of her body pressed upon him; her lids drooped over her eyes as her head leaned against his neck.

"I think you are tired and very sleepy," he repeated, pinching the glowing arm in its transparent muslin sleeve.

"If the Sahib says so, I must be," responded Saidie quite simply.

"Come, then, and sleep," he said in her ear, and they went upstairs.

Saidie gave a little cry of delight as they entered together the rose-filled room, and beyond its soft shaded lights she saw the great flashing planets in the dark sky.

"This is a different and a better home for love than we had last night," said Hamilton softly, as he closed the door.

A great peace reigned all round them. Within and without the bungalow there was no sound. The lights burned steadily and subdued, the sweet scent of the flowers hung in the air like a silent benediction upon them.

He put his arm round her, and felt her tremble excessively as his hand unfastened the clasp of her tunic. He stopped, surprised.

"Why do you tremble so? Are you afraid of me?" he asked, looking down upon her, all the tenderness and strength of a great passion in his eyes.

"No, no," she returned passionately, "I tremble because great waves of happiness rush over me at your touch. I cannot tell you what I feel, Sahib; the love and happiness within me is breaking me into fragments."

"Then you must break in my arms," he murmured back softly, drawing her into his embrace, "so that I shall not lose even one of them."

* * * * *

In the morning a flood of sunlight rushing into the room through the open windows, bringing with it the gay chatter of birds, roused the lovers. Hamilton opened his eyes first, and, lifting his head from the pillow, looked down upon Saidie still asleep beside him. In the rich mellow light of the room her loveliness glowed under his eyes like a jewel held in the sun. He hardly drew his breath, looking down upon her. Her heavy hair, full of deep purplish shades, and with the wave in it not unusual in the Asiatic, was pushed off the pale, pure bronze of the forehead, on which were drawn so perfectly the long-sweeping Oriental brows. The nose, delicately straight, with its proud high-arched nostrils, and the tiny upper lip, led the eye on to the finely-carved Eastern mouth, of which the lips now were softly, firmly folded in repose. How exquisitely Nature had fashioned those lips, putting more elaborate work in those lines and curves of that one feature than in the whole of an ordinary English face. Hamilton hung over her, filled with a passion of tenderness, watching the gentle breath move softly the warm column of bronze throat and raise the soft, full breast.

Passion, in its highest phase, is indeed the supreme gift of the gods. In giving it to a mortal for once they forget their envy: for once they raise him to their level; for that once they grant him divinity.

Hamilton now marvelled at himself. The whole fruit of his forty years of life - all that accomplished work, success, wealth, rewarded worth, satisfied ambition, all the pleasures his youth, his health and strength, and powers had always brought him, crushed together - could not equal this: the charm and ecstasy with which he gazed down on this warm beauty of the flesh beside him.

And yet he knew that it was not really in that flesh, not even in that beauty, that lay the delight. It was in himself, in his own intense desire, and the gratification of it, that the joy had birth; and if the gods give not this desire, no matter what else they give, it is useless.

The girl might have been as lovely, Hamilton himself, and all the circumstances the same, yet waking thus he might have been but the ordinary poor, cold, clay-like mortal a man usually is. But the great desire for this beauty that had flamed up within him, now in its possession, gave him that fervour and fire, those wings to his soul, that seemed to make him divine. It was for him one of those moments for which men live a life-time, as he indeed had done, but they repay him when they come. To some, they come never. To these life must indeed be dark.

Suddenly the girl opened her eyes; the fire in his bent upon her seemed to electrify and thrill her into life, and with a little murmur of delight she stretched up her rounded arms to him.

At breakfast Hamilton regretted he should have to leave her all day; what would she do?

"You must not think of it, Sahib," she answered. "Have I not the garden? I shall be quite happy. I shall sing all day long to the flowers about my lord, and count the minutes till he comes back."

The office did not attract Hamilton at all that day, yet he felt it was better to attend there as usual, to make no break in his usual routine.

Scandal there was sure to be, sooner or later, about his desert-bungalow, but at least it was better not to give to the scandal-mongers the power to say he had neglected his duties. Yet he lingered over his departure, and took her many times into his arms to kiss her before he went, keeping his impatient Arab waiting at the door. He would not use the camel again this morning, but left it resting in its corner of the compound beneath the palms.

After Hamilton had gone, Saidie stepped through the long window into the verandah, full of green light, completely shaded as it was by the giant convolvulus that spread all over it. The chetai crushed softly under her feet, and she went on slowly to the end where it opened to the compound. Here she stood for a moment gazing into the wilderness of beauty of mingled sun and shade before her.

Against the dazzling blue of the sky the branches of the palms stood out in gleaming gold, throwing their light shade over the masses of crimson and white and yellow roses that rioted together beneath. Groves of the feathery bamboo drooped their delicate stems in the fervent, sweet-scented heat, over the white, thick-lipped lilies, from one to other of which passed languidly on velvet wings great purple butterflies.

The pomegranate trees made a fine parade of their small, exquisite scarlet flowers, and pushed them upwards into the sparkling sunlight through the veils of white starry blossoms of the jessamine that climbed over and trailed from every tree in the compound.

The girl went forward dreaming. How completely, superbly

happy she was! And she had nothing but the gifts of Nature, such as she, the kindly one, gives to the gay bird swinging on the bough, the butterfly on the flower, the deer springing on the hills: health and youth, beauty and love.

These only were hers; nothing that man ordinarily strives for - neither wealth nor fame, fine houses, costly garments, jewels, slaves, power; none of these were hers. Over her body hung simply a muslin tunic worth a few annas; of the garden in which she stood not a flower belonged to her, no weight of jewels lay on her happy heart. She had no name; she was only a dancing-girl from the Deccan. With the animals she shared that wonderful kingdom of joy that they possess: their food and mate secured, their vigorous health bounding in their limbs, their beauty radiant in their perfect bodies.

Are they not the Lords of Creation in the sense that they are lords of joy? Man is the slave of the earth, doomed by his own vile lusts to bondage of the most dismal kind. All of those gifts that Nature gives, and from which alone can be drawn happiness, he tramples beneath his feet, putting his neck under the yoke of ceaseless toil, striving for things which in the end bring neither peace nor joy.

All within the compound under the reign of Nature rejoiced. The parroquets swung on the trees, and the butterflies floated from the marble whiteness of the lily's cloisters to the deep, warm recesses of the rose, and the dancing-girl walked singing through the sparkling, scented air thinking of her lord.

Hamilton, speeding down the dusty, burning road to his office in the native city, felt a strange bounding of his heart as his thoughts clung to the low, white bungalow amongst the palms outside the station, and all that it held for him.

He went through his work that day with a wonderful energy, born of the new life within him. Nothing fatigued, nothing worried him. The court-house air did not oppress him. He heard the pleadings and made his decisions with ease and promptitude. His patience, gentleness, his clearness and force of brain were wonderful. The whole electricity of his body was satisfied: the man was perfectly well and perfectly happy. Who cannot work under such conditions? In the evening his horse was brought round, and with a wild leaping of the heart he swung himself into the saddle. The animal felt instantly the elation of his master, and at once broke into a canter; as this was not checked, he threw up his lovely head, and as Hamilton turned across the plain, let himself go in a long gallop towards where the palms glowed living gold against the rose-hued sky.

Hamilton had hardly passed through the white chick into the interior of the house before he heard the sound of bare feet upon the matting, and through the soft magnolia-scented, pinky gloom of the room, shaded from the sunset light, Saidie came and fell at his knees, taking his dusty hands and kissing them.

Hamilton lifted her up, and held her a little from him, that he might feast his eyes on the delicate beautiful carving of the lips, and on the great velvet eyes, soft, round throat, and breasts swelling so warmly lovely under the transparent gauze.

Then he crushed her up in his arms close to his breast, and carried her to their own room with the golden and green chicks all round it, where the servants did not come without a summons. The garland she had twisted on her head smelt sweetly of roses, and the masses of her silky hair of sandal-wood; her soft lips, that knew so well instinctively the art of kissing, were on his; the warm, tender arms clasped his neck. All the way that he carried her she murmured little words of passion in his ear.

After dinner the servants carried chairs for them into the verandah, with a small table laden with drinks and sweetmeats, that they might sit and watch the moon rising behind the palms in the compound, and see the hot silver light pour slowly through their exquisite branches and foliage.

"How did you amuse yourself all day?" he asked her as she sat on his knee, his arm round the flexible, supple waist pulsating under the silky web of her tunic.

"I was so happy. I had so much to do, so much to think of," she answered, gazing back into his eyes bent upon her, and eagerly drawing in their fire. "I wandered in the compound and made garland after garland, then I sang to my rabab and practised my dancing. In the heat I went in and slept on my lord's bed dreaming of him - ah! how I dreamt of him!" She broke off sighing, and those sighs fanned the blazing fires in the man's veins.

"You were quite contented, then, with your day?"

"How could I not be contented when I had my lord to think about, his love of last night, his love of the coming night?"

Hamilton sighed and smiled at the same time.

"English wives need more than that to make them content," he answered.

"English wives," repeated Saidie, with her laugh like the sound of a golden bell; "what do they know of love?"

"Not much certainly, I think," replied Hamilton.

For a moment the vision of a thin blonde face, with its expression of sour discontent, rose before him. What had he not given that woman - what had she not demanded? Extravagant clothes to deck out her tall lean body, a carriage to drive her here and there, a mansion to live in, all the money he could gain by constant work - these things she demanded because she was his wife, and he had given them, and yet she was always discontented, simply because she was one of those women who do not know desire nor the delight of it. This one had nothing but that divine gift, and it made all her life joy.

"Dance for me now in the cool," murmured Hamilton in the little fine curved ear with the rose-bud just over it.

Saidie slipped off his knee, and fastening the little gilt link at her neck more securely, drew her soft filmy garment more closely to her, and commenced to dance before him in the screened verandah, with the hot moonlight, filtered through the delicate tracery; of innumerable leaves falling on her smooth, warm-tinted body.

To please him, to please him, her lord, her owner, her king: it was the one passion in her thoughts, and it flowed through every limb and muscle, glowed in her eyes, quivered on her parted lips, and made each movement a miracle of sweet sinuous grace.

The soft, hot night passed minute by minute, the scents of a thousand flowers mingled together in the still violet air. Some white night-moths came and fluttered round the exquisite form on whose rounded contours the light played so softly, and Hamilton lay back in his chair, silent, absorbed, hardly drawing his breath through his lungs, shaken by the nervous beating of his heart. Motionless he lay there, almost breathless, for the wine of life was in all his veins, mounting to his head, intoxicating him.

"I am very tired; may I stop now?" came at last in a low murmur from the curved lips so sweetly smiling at him, and the whole soft body drooped like a flower with fatigue. Hamilton opened his arms wide. She saw how the fresh colour glowed in the handsome cheek, how his splendid neck swelled as the red deer's in November, how the dark eyes blazed upon her.

"Come to me," he commanded, and she flew to his arms as the love-bird flies upward to her mate in the pomegranate tree.

CHAPTER III

For three months Hamilton and Saidie lived in the white bungalow in the palms, and drank of the wine of life together, and were happy in the overwhelming intoxication it gives.

For three months Saidie lived there, never going beyond the precincts of the house and the palace of flowers that was the compound.

Why should she leave them? What had she to gain by going out into the dusty way? What had she to seek? Her garden of Eden, her Paradise, was here. She was too wise to go beyond its limits.

Pedlars and merchants of all sorts brought their best and richest wares to her, and Hamilton sat by her in the verandah, commanding her to buy all that pleased her, though she protested she needed nothing.

Jewels for her neck, and gold anklets and bracelets, and robes and sweetmeats were laid out before her. Only the best of the bazaar was brought, and of this again only the best was chosen. And when Hamilton was not there she walked from room to room singing, clothed in purple silken gauze, with his jewels blazing on her breast, his kisses still burning on her lips. Then she would take her rabab and play to the listening flowers, or practise her dancing, the source of his pleasure, or lie in the noonday heat on the edge of the bubbling spring that rose up in the moss under the boughain-villia and look towards the

East and dream of his home-coming. What did she want more?

Hamilton now lived the enchanted life of one who is wholly absorbed in a secret passion. He was wise - more wise than men generally are - and made no effort to parade his treasure. This wonderful exotic, this flower of happiness, that bloomed so vividly in the dark, secluded recesses of his heart, how did he know that the destructive heat and light of publicity might not fade and sear its marvellous petals? He told no one of his life; took no one out into the desert with him, to the bungalow among the palms.

He was away a great deal. His work and certain social duties claimed a large part of his day, and during all that time he had to leave her alone with her flowers, but this gave him no anxiety. It was not a dangerous experiment, as it always is to leave a European woman alone. He knew that Saidie, the Oriental, would spend the whole time dreaming of him, longing for him, singing to the flowers of him, talking to her women-attendants of him, filling the whole garden and house with his image till the longed-for moment of his return.

And to Hamilton, full of unspoiled life and vigour, this security, this certainty of her complete fidelity was a wondrous charm.

Unlike a man of jaded passions, who requires his love to be constantly stimulated by the fear of imminent loss, Hamilton, full of unused strength, and thirsty after the joy of life, now that the cup was offered him, drank of it naturally and with ecstasy, needing no salt and bitter olives of jealousy between the draughts.

For years he had longed for love and happiness: at last he had found both, and with simple, uncavilling thankfulness he clasped them to his breast and held them there, content.

Saturday and Sunday were their great days. Hamilton left the

Victoria Cross

office at two on Saturday afternoon, and was back at the bungalow by five.

They went to bed early that night, and rose on the Sunday morning with the first glimmer of dawn. Everything would be prepared overnight for a day's excursion and picnic in the desert, which Saidie particularly delighted in.

The great brown camel, fat and sleek like all Hamilton's animals, and with an enormous weight of rich hair on his supple neck, would be kneeling waiting for them below in the dewy compound, while the early tender light stole softly through the palms; and they would mount and go swinging out through the great open spaces of the desert, full of delicate white light, towards the sister-oasis of Dirampir, where masses of cocoanut palms grew round a set of springs, and waved their branches joyfully as they drew in the salt nourishment of the air from the amethystine sea not fifty miles distant.

Into the shelter of these palms they would come as the first great golden wave of light from the climbing sun broke over the desert, and, descending from the camel, walk about in the groves by the spring, and select a place for boiling their kettle and having their breakfast. The long ride in the keen air of the morning gave them great appetites, and they enjoyed it in the whole joyous beauty of the scene round them. The palm branches over them grew gold against the laughing blue of the sky, a thousand shafts of sunlight pierced through the fan-like tracery, the golden orioles at play darted, chasing each other from bough to bough, the spring bubbled its cool musical notes beside them, and the sense of the blighting heat of the ravening desert round them seemed to accentuate the beauty of the peace and shade in the oasis.

Saidie enjoyed these days beyond everything, and would sit singing at the foot of a palm, weaving a garland of white clematis for Hamilton's handsome head as it rested on her lap.

No English people ever came to the oasis; as a matter of fact, the English generally do avoid the best and most beautiful spots in or near an Indian station; but the place was greatly beloved by the natives who came there to doze and dream, play, sing, and weave garlands in the usual harmless manner in which a native takes his pleasure. Looking at them standing or sitting in their harmonious groups against a background of golden light and delicate shade, Hamilton often thought how well this scene compared with that of the Britisher taking a holiday - Hampstead Heath, for instance, with its noisy drunkenness, its spirit of hateful spite, its ill-used animals, its loathsome language. The Oriental endeavours to enjoy himself, and his method is generally peaceful and poetic: the singing of songs, the weaving of garlands, and the letting alone of others. The Briton's idea of enjoying himself is extremely simple; it consists solely in annoying his neighbours.

To see a handsome English Sahib here was to the habitual frequenters of the oasis something rather remarkable, but these people are early taught the custody of the eyes and to mind their own business. Therefore Hamilton and Saidie were not troubled by offensive stares, or in any other way. All there were free, gathered to enjoy themselves, each man in his own way; and the natives in their gay colours added to the beauty, without disturbing the peace of the scene, much as the bright-plumaged birds that flitted from tree to tree absorbed in their own affairs.

How Hamilton enjoyed those long, calm, golden hours - the golden hours of Asia, so full of the enchantment of rich light and colour, soft beauty before the eyes, sweet scent of the jessamine in the nostrils, the warbling of birds, and Saidie's love songs in his ears!

Not till the glorious rose of the sunset diffused itself softly in the luminous sky, and all the desert round them grew pink, and the shadows of the palms long in the oasis, and the great planets above them burst blazing into view into the still rose-hued sky, did they rise from the side of the spring and begin to think of their homeward ride. And what a delight it was that night ride home through the majestic silence of the desert, where their own hearts' beating and the soft footfall of the camel were the only sounds! the wild flash of planet and star, and sometimes the soft glimmer of the rising moon, their only light! Eros, the god of passion, seated with them on the camel, their only companion!

To Saidie, cradled in his arms, looking upwards to his face above her, its beauty distinct in the soft light, feeling his heart beating against her side, it seemed as if her happiness was too great for the human frame to bear, as if it must dissolve, melt into nothingness, against his breast, and her spirit pass into the great desert solitudes, dispersed, almost annihilated, in the agony and ecstasy of love.

Week after week passed lightly by in their brilliant setting, the hours on their winged feet danced by, and these two lived independent of all the world, wrapped up in their own intimate joy.

One morning, just as he was about to leave the bungalow, he heard Saidie's voice calling him back. He turned and saw her smiling face hanging over the stair-rail above him. He remounted the stairs, and she drew him into their room. Her face was radiant, her eyes blazed with light as she looked at him.

"I have something to tell you, Sahib! I could not let you go without saying it. Only think! is not Allah good to me? I am to be the mother of the Sahib's child," and she fell on her knees, kissing his hands in a passion of joy. Hamilton stood for the moment silent. He was startled, unprepared for her words, unused to the wild joy with which the Oriental woman hails a coming life.

Her message carried a certain shock to him: it augured change; and his happiness had been so perfect, so absolute, what would change, any change, even if wrought by the divine Hand itself, mean to him but loss?

Saidie, terrified at his silence, looked up at him wildly.

"What have I done? Is not my lord pleased?" Her accent was one of the acutest fear.

Hamilton bent down and raised her to his breast.

"Dearest one, light of my soul, how could I not be pleased?" and he kissed her many times on the lips, and on the soft upper arm that pressed his throat, and on her neck, till even she was satisfied.

"Come and sit with me for a moment that I may tell you all," she said. Hamilton sat beside her on the bed, and she told him many things that an Englishwoman would never say, nor would it enter into her mind to conceive them.

Hamilton was greatly moved as he sat listening. The wonderful imagery, the vivid language in which she clothed her pure joyous thoughts appealed to his own poetic, artistic habit of mind.

On his way across the desert to the city, Hamilton pondered deeply over the news and the girl's unaffected joy. Since all those whispered confidences poured into his ear while they sat side by side on the bed, the throb of jealousy he had first felt at her words had passed away. Saidie had made it so clear to him that her joy was not so great at being the mother of a child as that she was to be the mother of *his* child, and similarly Hamilton felt in all his being a curious thrill at the thought that his child was hers, that this new life was created in and of her life that had become so infinitely dear to him.

He was glad now that his wife had refused to have a child. The bitter pain he had felt then, those years ago, how little he had thought it was to be the parent of this present joy. Now the woman he loved as he had loved no other would be the one to bear his child. Still the thought of the suffering the mother would go through depressed his sensitive mind, and the idea of the risk to her life that came suddenly into his brain made him turn white to the lips as he rode in the hot sunlight. Such intense happiness as he had known for the last three months can turn a brave man into a coward. For a moment he faced the horrid thought that had come to him - Saidie dead! And the whole brilliant plain, laughing sky, and dancing sunlight and waving palms became black to him. To go back to that dreary existence of nothingness of his former life, after once having known the delight that this bright, eager, ardent love, these delicate little clinging hands had made for him, would be impossible.

"No," he murmured to himself, "if she goes, then it's a snuff out for me too. I have never cared for life except as she has made it for me."

And the cloud rolled off him a little as he met the idea of his own death. Besides, Saidie had declared so positively that she could come to no harm, that it would all be pure delight, that pain and suffering could not exist for her in such a matter since she would be all joy in making him this gift, that gradually he grew calmer as he thought over her words.

"But I didn't want any change," he burst out a little later, talking to the still golden air round him. "Confound it! I was perfectly happy. How impossible it is to keep anything as it is in this world! All our actions drag in upon us their consequences so fast! There is no getting away from this horrible change, no enjoying one's happiness peacefully when one has obtained it."

When he arrived at his office in the city he found that a far heavier cloud had arisen on his horizon than that created by Saidie's words. The English mail was in, and a long thin envelope, impressed with a much-hated handwriting, faced him on the top of the pile of his correspondence as he entered.

He picked it up and opened it.

"DEAR FRANK, - You often used to invite me to come to India, and I have really at last made up my mind to. I am coming out by next month's boat to stay with you for a time. I have been very much run down in health lately, and my doctor says a sea-voyage and six months in India will be first-rate for me. I hope you have a nice comfortable house and good servants.

- Yours affectionately, JANE."

Hamilton stared at the letter savagely as he put it down before him on the table, a sort of grim smile breaking slowly over his face. He felt convinced that in some way his wife had learned of his new-found happiness, and that had given birth to her sudden desire to visit India after twenty years of persistent refusal to do so. He sat motionless for a long time, then stretched out his hand for an English telegraph form and wrote on it -

"Regret unable to receive you now. Defer visit. FRANK."

He did not for one moment think that his wife would obey his injunction, or that his wire would have the least effect on her; but he wished to have a good ground to stand on when she arrived, and he declined to receive her. His teeth set for a moment as he thought of the interview.

"This is a sort of wind-up day of my happiness," he muttered, as he took his place at the office table. "Well, I suppose no one could expect such pleasure as I have had these last three months to continue; but, whatever happens, Saidie and I will stick together." He sat musing for a moment, staring with unseeing eyes at the pile of work in front of him.

"Saidie, my Saidie! I shall never part from her; therefore I can never part from my happiness." He smiled a little at the play on the words, and then commenced his day's labours.

That evening, when he returned, Saidie noticed at once the

depression in his usually gay, bright manner. When they were alone at dinner she laid her hand on his.

"What has darkened the light of my lord's countenance?" she asked softly.

Hamilton drew from his pocket his wife's letter, and laid it beside her plate.

"Can you read that, Saidie? If so, you will know all about it."

The girl leaned one elbow on the table and bent over the letter, studying it. She had been trying hard to improve herself in the language, of which she knew already something, and with Oriental quickness, had acquired much in the past three months. She made out the sense now easily enough.

"This lady is a wife of yours?" she said quickly, with a swift upward glance at him, when she had finished reading the letter.

Hamilton laughed a little.

"She was my wife till I saw you, Saidie. No one is my wife now, nor ever will be, but you."

A soft glow of supreme pleasure and pride lighted up Saidie's great lustrous eyes. She bent her head and put her soft lips to his hand.

"Have you forbidden this wife to come to you?" she asked after a minute.

"Yes, I have; but she will come all the same. English wives think it foolish to obey their husbands."

He laughed sardonically, and Saidie looked bewildered and horrified.

*   *   *   *   *

A month later, a long, lean woman sat in a deck chair on board an Indian liner as it crossed the enchanted waters of the Indian Ocean. Enchanted, for surely it is some magician's touch that makes these waters such a rich and glorious blue! How they roll so gently, full of majestic beauty, crested with sunlight, under the ships they carry so lightly! How the gold light leaps over them, how the azure sky above laughs down to their tranquil mirror! How the gleaming flying-fish rise in their glinting cloud, whirl over them, and then softly disappear into their mysterious embrace!

The long, lean woman saw none of the magic round her. Her dull, boiled-looking eyes gazed through the soft sunlight without seeing it. In her lap lay a thin foreign letter and a telegram, together with a copy of "Anna Lombard" that she was reading with the strongest disapproval. She picked up the letter and glanced through it again, though she knew it nearly by heart, especially one passage:

> "Your husband is leading such a life here! He has built a wonderful white marble palace in the desert for an Egyptian dancing-girl. They say it's a sort of Antony and Cleopatra over again, and she goes about loaded with jewels and golden chains. I don't know if you are getting your allowance regularly, but I should think your husband is pretty well ruining himself. I never saw a man so changed. He used to be so melancholy, but now he is as bright as possible, and looks so well and handsome. I hear the woman is expecting a child, and they are both as pleased as they can be. I hear all about it, as our cook's cousin is sister to the ayah your husband hired for the woman, and my ayah gets it all from our cook. I really should, my dear, come out and look into the matter, as after a time he will probably want to stop sending home his pay."

The thin sheet fell into the woman's lap again, and she seemed to ponder deeply. Then she read Hamilton telegram again -

"Regret unable to receive you now. Defer visit," and a disagreeable laugh broke from her thick, colourless lips.

"I will go out and see her first," she thought, smoothing down with a large, bony hand the folds of her rather prim white cambric dress. She was a very stupid woman, and not a passionate one; therefore the agony of pain of a loving, jealous wife was quite unknown to her. But she was malignant, as such people usually are. She loved making other people uncomfortable in a general way, and taking away from them anything she could that they valued. She also felt a peculiar curiosity such as those who cannot feel passion themselves have usually about the intense happiness it gives to others. The picture of this other woman, who had found joy apparently in the arms she herself years ago had thrust aside, interested her profoundly. She told herself that this Egyptian loved Hamilton's money, but some instinct within her held her back from believing this.

The little bit about the child went deeply into her mind. It rested there like an arrow-head, and her thoughts grew round it. When the ship came into port a week or two later, Mrs. Hamilton was one of the first passengers to land, and after careful enquiries and well-bestowed tips she was expeditiously conveyed by ticker-gharry[1] and sedan chair across the desert to the bungalow at Deira. She was considerably pleased on seeing that the white marble palace resolved itself into an ordinary white bungalow, but the garden, was unutterably lovely, and, as she saw in a moment, represented something quite unusual in cost and care.

[Footnote 1: Hired carriage.]

It was just high noon when she arrived, and she thankfully escaped from the suffocating heat and glare of the desert into the cool shaded hall, and gave her card with a throb of spiteful elation to the butler.

The Oriental servant read the name, and hurried with the card to his mistress's room. On hearing of the arrival of the Mem-Sahib, Saidie descended from the upper room, where she had been lying in the noonday heat, and, pushing aside the great golden chick that swung before the drawing-room entrance, went in.

Her dress was of the most exquisite Indian muslin that Hamilton could obtain, heavily and wonderfully embroidered in gold, and peacocks' eyes of vivid deep blue and green; her feet were bare, for Hamilton, in his revolt from English ways, had kept up Oriental traditions as far as possible in the clothing of his new mistress, and weighty anklets of solid gold gleamed beneath the border of her skirt. Round the perfect column of her neck, full and stately as the red deer's, were twisted great strings of pearls, throwing their pale irridescent greenish hue onto the velvet skin. Above the splendour of her dress rose the regal and lovely face, its delicate carving and the marvel of its dark, flashing, enquiring eyes vividly striking in the clear mellow light of the room.

Mrs. Hamilton, dressed in a plain, grey alpaca dress, rather hot and dusty after her long drive, sat on one of the low divans awaiting her. As Saidie entered, the glory of her youth and beauty struck upon the seated woman like a heavy blow, under which she started to her feet and stood for a second, involuntarily shrinking.

"Salaam, be seated," murmured Saidie, indicating a fauteuil near the one on which she sank herself.

Mrs. Hamilton came forward, her hands closing and unclosing spasmodically in their grey silk gloves, and sat down again, her eyes riveted on the other's face.

"Do you know who I am?" she said at last in a stifled voice.

Saidie smiled faintly; one of those liquid, lingering smiles that made Hamilton's heaven.

"Yes, I know; you are Mem Sahib Hamilton, the first, the old wife.".

Saidie, according to her own Eastern ideas, was in the position of a superior receiving an unfortunate inferior. She was the latest acquired - the darling, the reigning queen - confronted with the poor cast-off, old, unattractive first wife; and being of a nature equally noble as the type of her beauty, she felt it incumbent on her, in such a situation, to treat the unfortunate with every consideration, gentleness, and tenderness.

The British matron's views of the relative positions of first and subsequent wives differs, however, from Saidie's, and Mrs. Hamilton's face grew purple as she heard Saidie's answer, and some faint comprehension of Saidie's view was borne in upon her.

"Where is my husband?" she demanded fiercely.

"The Sahib is in the city to-day," returned Saidie calmly. How odious they were, these Englishwomen, with their short skirts and big boots, and red, hot faces, with great black straw houses over them, and their curt manners, and the impertinent way they spoke of their lords!

"When will he be back?" pursued the other, sharply.

Saidie glanced towards the clock.

"In a few hours; perhaps more. He returns at sunset."

"And what do you do all day, shut up by yourself?" questioned her visitor, with a sort of contemptuous surprise.

"I think of him," returned Saidie, quite simply, with a sort of proud pleasure that made the Englishwoman stare incredulously.

"Silly little fool!" she ejaculated, with a harsh, disdainful laugh.

"Does he give you all those things, and dress you up like that?" she added, staring at the pearls on Saidie's neck.

"He has given me everything I have," she replied, seriously.

That Hamilton was wasting his substance on another went home far more keenly to his lawful wife than that he was wasting his love on the same. She got up, and went close to the girl, with a face of fury.

"They are all mine! I should like to drag them off you! Do you understand that an Englishman's money belongs to his wife, and *I* am his wife? You! What are you? He belongs to me, and, whatever you may think, I can take him from you. By our laws he must come back to me."

Saidie rose and faced the angry woman unmoved.

"No law on earth can make a man stay with a woman he does not love," she said calmly, "nor take him from one he does. You must know little, or you would know that love is stronger than all law. I give you leave to withdraw. Salaam."

And she herself moved slowly backwards towards the hanging chick, passed through it, and was gone, leaving the Englishwoman alone in the room.

*   *   *   *   *

Three hours later Hamilton, sitting in his own private office, surrounded with papers, started suddenly as he heard a well-known and hated voice say, outside the door.

"Thanks, I'll go in myself."

The next minute the door had opened and his wife stood before him. He sat in silence, regarding her.

"Well, Frank, I suppose you were expecting me? You saw the

boat came in, doubtless. You don't look particularly pleased to see me!"

There was only one chair in the room, and Hamilton remained seated. His wife stood in front of him.

"I do not know of any reason why I should be pleased, do you?" he said calmly, gazing at her with eyes full of concentrated hostility.

"No, considering you've got that black woman up at your house, I don't suppose you do want your wife back very badly; but I've come to stay, my dear fellow, some time, so you've got to make the best of it."

"You will not stay with me," returned Hamilton quietly. His face was very white, his eyes had become black as they looked at her. One hand played idly with a paper-knife on his table.

"And a nice scandal there'll be when I go to stay at the hotel here, and it's known I'm your wife, and you are living out in the desert with a woman from the bazaar!"

"The fear of scandal has long since ceased to regulate my life," answered Hamilton calmly. "Be good enough to make your interview short; I have a great deal of work to-day."

"You are a devil!" replied the woman, white, too, now with impotent rage, "to desert your own wife for that filthy native woman. I - "

But Hamilton had sprung to his feet; his face was blazing; he seized his wife's wrists in both hands.

"Be quiet," he said, in a low tone of such fury that she cowered beneath it. "One word more and I shall *kill* you; do you understand?"

Then he raised one hand and brought it down on his gong.

Instantly two stalwart, bronze giants, his chuprassis, entered the room and stood by the door.

"Take this woman out, and keep her out," he said to them. "Never let her in again. She annoys me."

The chuprassis put their hands to their foreheads, and then impassively approached the Englishwoman. She looked at her husband wildly as they took her arms.

"Frank! you will not surely -" she expostulated. "Your own wife!" and she struggled to release her arms.

Hamilton waved his hand, and the natives forced her to the door. For a moment she seemed inclined to scream and struggle. Then her face changed. A look of intense malevolence came over it. She walked between the men quietly to the door. As she passed through it, she looked back.

"You and she shall regret this," she said. Then the door shut, and Hamilton was alone.

He sat down, collapsed in his chair. Oh, how could he free himself from this millstone at his neck? What relief could he gain anywhere? To what power appeal? He could keep her out of his house, out of his office, but not out of his life. She had come here with the deliberate intention of wrecking that, and she would succeed probably, for she would have the blind, hideous force of conventional morality on her side. She would destroy his life - that life till lately so valueless to him; that dreary stretch made barren so many years by her hateful influence, but which, in spite of it, at Saidie's touch, had now bloomed into a garden of flowers. The thought of Saidie strengthened him. It was true that his wife would probably succeed in breaking up his life here from the conventional and social point of view, and he would be obliged most likely to give up his appointment; but he had a small independent income, and on that he and Saidie could still live together. They would go to Ceylon or to Malabar. Perhaps also he could make money otherwise than officially. Wherever he went his wife would probably pursue him, intent on making his life a misery. Still, Fortune might favour him; he and Saidie might in time reach some corner of the world where their remorseless tracker would lose trace of them. Perhaps to go to England at once and obtain a legal separation would be the best plan, but then it was winter in England now, and he could not with advantage take Saidie to England in winter, for fear his exotic Eastern flower would fade in the northern winds.

His thoughts wandered from point to point, and the minutes passed unheeded. His papers lay untouched, scattered on the floor. The chuprassi brought in from time to time a note, laid it on the table and withdrew. Hamilton noticed nothing; he sat still, thinking.

Meanwhile Mrs. Hamilton had been driven to the hotel, where she engaged very modest quarters and ordered luncheon. While waiting for this she went out into the balcony before her windows, and looked with gloomy eyes into the sunny, laughing splendour of the Eastern afternoon. At the side of the hotel was a luxuriant garden, and the palms and sycamores growing there threw a light shade into the sunny street just below her window; the sky overhead stretched its eternal Eastern blue, and the pigeons wheeled joyfully in and out the eaves in the clear sparkling air, or descended to the pools in the garden to bathe, with incessant cooing. Up and down the road passed the white bullocks with their laden carts, and the gaily-dressed Turkish sweet-meat sellers went by crooning out songs descriptive of their wares, pausing under the shade of the garden to look up at the English Mem-Sahib in the balcony. She leant her arms on the rail, and looked out on the gay scene with unseeing eyes. "Beast!" she muttered at intervals, and her hard-lined face crimsoned and paled by turns.

When her luncheon came in she returned to the room, took off her hat and looked in the glass. The narrow, selfish, petty emotions of twenty years were written all over her face in deep, hideous lines. The mass of yellow hair, newly-dyed, looked glaringly youthful and incongruous above it.

Burning with a sense of malevolent discontent and misery, she turned from the glass and hurried through her luncheon, then ordered it to be cleared away and writing materials to be brought in, and set herself with grim feverishness to the concoction of a long letter to the Commissioner. In it Hamilton's twenty years of patient fidelity, through which time he had regularly transmitted to her half his pay year by year were naturally not mentioned; her own refusal to live with him, her incessant demands for more money, her extravagance, her long, whining letters to him, her debts, her own life in town were, of course, also suppressed. In the letter she figured as the ardent, tender, anxious wife, arriving to find her abandoned husband wasting his substance on a black mistress. The visit to the cruel tyrant in his office was long dwelt on, and the whole closed with a pathetic appeal to the Commissioner to use his influence to restore her dearest boy to her arms. It was not a bad letter from the artist's and the liar's standpoint, and she read it through with a glow of satisfaction, sealed it up with a baleful smile of triumph, and then sounded the gong.

"Take this at once to the Commissioner Sahib," she said, handing the note to the servant, "and let me have some tea; also you can order me a carriage. I shall want to drive afterwards."

When the tea came, she thoroughly enjoyed it after her virtuous labours, and in the cool of the evening drove out to see the city.

*   *   *   *   *

That evening at dinner, seated at their table, laden with flowers, with the light from the heavy Burmese silver lamps falling on her lovely glowing face, and round bangle-laden arms, Saidie told Hamilton of the visit of the white Mem-Sahib. His face darkened and his lips set.

"So she came here, did she? Did she frighten you? attempt to hurt you?"

"Oh, no," returned Saidie; "not at all. Naturally she is very hurt, very sorry; no wonder she longs after the Sahib, and wishes to be taken back to his harem. I was very sorry for her. It is quite natural she should be jealous, of course," and Saidie rested one soft, silken skinned elbow on the table and leaned across the flowers, and her half-filled wine-glass, looking with tender liquid eyes earnestly at the face of her lord.

"The Sahib is so wonderful, so beautiful, so far above other men," she murmured, gazing upon him. "It is no wonder she is unhappy."

Hamilton smiled a little, looking back at her. He had indeed a singularly handsome face, with its straight, noble features and warm colour, and as he smiled the breast of the Eastern girl heaved; her heart seemed to rush out to him.

"Ah, Saidie! you do not understand English wives," he said gently, with a curious melancholy in his voice. "Love and worship such as you give me they think shameful and shocking. To love a man for himself, for his face, for his body is degrading. They are so pure, they love him only for his purse. They tell him to take his passion to dancing-girls like you. They hate to bear him children. They like to live in his house, be clothed at his expense, ride in his carriage, but they care little to sleep in his arms."

Saidie regarded him steadfastly, with eyes ever growing wider as she listened.

"I do not understand ..." she murmured at last, clasping both soft, supple hands across her breast, as if trying to mould herself into this new belief; "it is so hard to comprehend.... Surely it must be right to love one's lord, to bear him sons, to please him, to make him happy every hour, every minute of the day and night."

"Right?" returned Hamilton passionately, getting up from his seat and coming over to her. "Of course it is right! love such as yours is a divine gift to man, straight from the hands of God." He leaned his burning hands heavily on the delicately-moulded shoulders, looking down into her upturned face. How exquisite it was! its fine straight nose, its marvellously-carved mouth and short upper lip, its round, full chin, and midnight eyes beneath their great arching, sweeping brows!

"That woman is a fiend, one of the unnatural creatures our wretched European civilisation has made only to destroy the lives of men. Don't let us speak of her! never let us think of her! She is nothing to me. You are my world, my all. If she drives us away from here, there are other parts of the world for us. Separate us she never shall. Come! why should we waste our time even mentioning her name. Come with me into our garden. Darling! darling!"

He stooped over her, and on her lips pressed those kisses so long refused, uncared for by one woman, so priceless to this one, and almost lifted Saidie from the chair. She laughed the sweet low laughter of the Oriental woman, and went with him eagerly towards the verandah, and out into the compound where the roses slept in the warm silver light.

* * * * *

For two days nothing happened. Hamilton went as usual to his office for the day. At four he left, and, mounting his camel, went into the desert to the oasis in the palms.

On the third day he received a summons from the Commissioner, and went up to his house in the afternoon. His heart seethed with rage within him, but except for an unusual pallor in the clear warm skin, his face showed nothing as he entered the large, imposing drawing-room.

The Commissioner was a short, pompous little man, rather overshadowed by his grim raw-boned wife, and had under her strict guidance and training developed a stern admiration for conventional virtue, particularly in regard to conjugal relations. He rose and bowed as Hamilton entered, but did not offer to shake hands. Hamilton waited, erect, silent.

"Sit down, Mr. Hamilton." Hamilton sat down. "Er - I - ah - have received what I may term a painful - yes, a very painful communication, and er - I may say at once it refers to you and your concerns in a most distressing manner - most distressing."

The Commissioner coughed and waited. Hamilton remained silent. The Commissioner fidgeted, crossed his knees, uncrossed them again, then turned on him suddenly. The Indian climate is trying to the temper; it means many pegs, and small control of the passions.

"Damn you, sir!" he broke out fiercely. "What the devil do you mean by keeping a black woman in your house, and sending your wife to the hotel here?"

He was purple and furious; in his hand he crushed Mrs. Hamilton's beautiful composition.

"She tells me you called in natives to throw her out of your office: it's disgraceful! Upon my word it is; it's scandalous! And you sent her to the hotel! I never heard of such a thing!"

"Mrs. Hamilton came out uninvited, in defiance of my express wishes, and on her arrival I told her she could not stay with me," returned Hamilton quietly. "Whether she went to the hotel or not, I don't know."

"But your wife, damn it all, your wife, has a right to stay with you if she chooses; naturally she would come to you, and you can't turn her out in this way."

"She has long ago forfeited all rights as my wife," replied Hamilton calmly, in a low tone, with so much weight in it that the Commissioner looked at him keenly.

"Why don't you get a divorce or a separation then?" he asked abruptly. "Do the thing decently - not have her out like this, and make a scandal all over the station."

"I know of no grounds for a divorce," returned Hamilton. "There are many ways of breaking the marriage vows other than infidelity. I married Mrs. Hamilton twenty years ago, and for those twenty years she has practically refused to live with me. For twenty years I have remitted half my income to her every year. During that time I have many times asked her to join me here, sought a reconciliation always to be refused. Recently I found another interest; the moment my wife discovered this, she came out with the sole purpose of annoying me. I have come to the conclusion that twenty years' fidelity to a woman without reward is enough. I shall not alter my life now to suit Mrs. Hamilton."

The Commissioner was silent. He was quite sure Hamilton was speaking the truth, and in reality, in the absence of Mrs. Commissioner, he felt all his sympathies go with him. But his wife's careful training and his official position put other words than his mind dictated into his mouth.

"Well, well," he said at last, "we can't go into all that. You and your wife must arrange your matters somehow between you. But there can't be a scandal like this going on. You, a married man, living with a native woman, and your wife out here at the hotel! Something must be done to make things look all right - must be done," and he knitted his brows, looking crossly at Hamilton from under them.

Hamilton shrugged his shoulders.

"You'd better give up this native woman," snapped the Commissioner.

Hamilton smiled. His was such an expressive face, it told more clearly the feelings than most impassive English faces, and there was that in the smile that held the Commissioner's gaze;

and the two men sat staring at each other in silence.

After some moments the Commissioner spoke again but his tone was different.

"Hamilton, you know we all have to make sacrifices to our official position, to public opinion, to social usage. Ah! what a Moloch that is that we've created, it devours our best. Yes ... a Moloch!" he muttered half to himself, gazing on the floor.

"Still, it's there, and we all suffer equally in turn. I know what it is myself. I have been through it all." He stopped, gazing fixedly at the beautiful crimson roses in the pattern of his Wilton carpet. What visions swept before him of gleaming eyes and sweeping brows, ruthlessly blotted out by a large, raw-boned figure and face of aggressive chastity. "I am sorry for you, but there it is; whatever the rights of the case, you can't make a scandal like this."

"I am ready to resign my post if necessary," returned Hamilton; "I have enough to live on without my pay."

The Commissioner started, and looked at him.

"Is she so handsome as that?" he asked in a low tone, leaning a little forward. Mrs. Commissioner was not there, and he was forgetting officialdom.

Hamilton hesitated a moment. Then he drew from his pocket a photograph, taken by himself, of Saidie standing amongst her flowers.

The beautiful Eastern face, the lovely, youthful, sinuous figure, veiled in its slight, transparent drapery, taken by an artist and a lover in the clear, actinic Indian light, made an exquisite work of art. It lay in the hand of the Commissioner, and he gazed on it, remembering his long-past youth.

After a long time Hamilton broke the silence.

"Now, you know," he said at last, "why I am ready to resign my post rather than resign *that*; and it is not only her beauty that charms me, it is her devotion, her love.... Do you know, white or black, superior or inferior, these two women are not to be mentioned in one breath. The one you see there is a woman, the other is a fiend."

The Commissioner tried to look shocked, but failed; the smooth card still lay in his hand, the lovely image impressed on it smiled up at him.

"I don't know but what you are right," he muttered savagely as he handed it back to Hamilton. "These wives, damn 'em, seem to have no other mission but to make a man uncomfortable."

He got up and began to pace the room. He seemed to have forgotten Hamilton and the official *role* he himself had started to play. He seemed absorbed in his own thoughts - perhaps memories. Hamilton sat still, gazing at the card.

Half-an-hour later the interview came to an end. Hamilton went away to his office with a light heart, and a smile on his lips. The Commissioner had given him some of his own reminiscences, and Hamilton had sympathised. The two men had drifted insensibly onto common ground, and the Commissioner finally had promised to help Hamilton as far as he could. Hamilton was pleased. That he had merely been twisting a piece of straw, that would be bent into quite another shape when Mrs. Commissioner took it in hand, did not for the moment occur to him. That night Saidie danced for him in the moonlight, and afterwards ran from him swiftly, playing at hide-and-seek amongst the roses laughing, inviting his pursuit. In and out behind the great clumps of boughain-villia gleamed the lovely form, with hair unbound falling like a mantle to the waist. Through the pomegranate bushes the laughing face looked out at him, then swiftly vanished as he approached, and next a laugh and a flash of warm skin drew him to the bed of lilies where he overtook her, and they fell laughing on the mossy bank together. Wearied with dancing and running and laughter, she sank into his arms gladly, as Eve in the garden of Eden.

"Let us sleep here," she murmured, looking up to the palm branches over them defined against the lustrous sky.

"See how the lilies sleep round us!"

And that night they slept out in the moonlight.

CHAPTER IV

A month had gone by, and during that month, except for the time he was with Saidie in the bungalow, Hamilton, had he been less of a philosopher, would have been extremely uncomfortable.

The Commissioner's wife had completely and entirely espoused the cause of Mrs. Hamilton, and had insisted on her leaving the hotel and coming to stay with her. Everywhere that the Commissioner's wife went, riding or driving, Mrs. Hamilton accompanied her; and whenever he met the two women, his wife threw him a mild, reproachful glance of martyred virtue, while the Commissioner's wife glared upon him in stony wrath.

Hamilton took no notice of either glance, but passed them as if neither existed. The Commissioner looked miserably guilty whenever he encountered Hamilton's amused, penetrating eyes, and avoided him as much as possible. The Commissioner's house was completely shut to him; he never approached it now except on official business, and nearly every house in the station followed its example. The story of Mrs. Hamilton's woes and wrongs had spread all over the community, and proved a theme of delightful and never-ending interest to all the ladies of the station. They were unanimous in supporting her. Not one voice was raised in favour of Hamilton. He was a monster, a heartless libertine, given over to all sorts of terrible vices. Tales of the fearful doings in the desert bungalow, where Hamilton and Saidie lived the gay, bright, joyous life of two human beings, happily mated, as Nature intended all things to be, spread over the station, and the stony stare of the women upon Hamilton, when they met him, mingled insensibly with a shrinking horror that greatly amused him.

Nobody spoke to him except in his business capacity. Every one avoided him. He was practically ostracised. Mrs. Hamilton, on the other hand, went everywhere, and thoroughly enjoyed herself in the *role* of gentle forgiving martyr that she played to perfection. Being plain and unattractive to men, she was thoroughly popular with the women, and they were never tired of condoling with her on having such a brute of a husband. What more natural, poor dear! than that she should refuse to live with him in India, if the climate did not suit her? So unreasonable of him to expect it! The question of a family, too! why, what woman was there now who did not hate to have her figure spoiled, and object to be always in the sick-room and nursery? So natural that she did not wish those disagreeable passionate relationships: a man could not expect that sort of thing from his wife! And then the money, too! she had never had more than half his income all these twenty years! It seemed to them that she had been wonderfully good and resigned.

Such was the talk at the afternoon teas, and the married men at the club, coached by their wives, and being in the position of the fox who had lost his brush, and wished no other fox to retain his, condemned Hamilton quite as freely.

"It was beastly rough on his wife," they agreed, "to set up a black dancing-girl under her eyes."

Hamilton cared not at all for the social life of the station, and was greatly relieved by not having invitations to give or to answer. All that he regretted was the ultimate resignation of his post, which, he foresaw, would be the result of all this scandal sooner or later.

Saidie, with Oriental quickness, had soon grasped the whole situation, and had flung herself at his feet in a passion of tears, begging him to send her away or to kill her rather than let her presence make him unhappy. Hamilton had some difficulty in turning her mind from the resolve to kill herself by way of serving him; and it was only his solemn oath to her that she was the one single joy and happiness of his life, that with her in his arms he cared about nothing else, that if he lost her his life was at an end, which pacified and at last convinced her.

Another month went by, and Mrs. Hamilton began to tire of her position. She felt she was not making Hamilton half unhappy enough. She had had but one idea, and that was to separate him from Saidie, and in this she had failed. He had not even been turned out of his post. He had been expelled from the social life of the station; but she knew he would not feel that, that he would only welcome the greater leisure he had to spend in his Eden with *her*. To play the martyr for a time had been interesting, but its pleasure was beginning to wane; moreover, she could not stay permanently with the Commissioner's wife. She grew restless: she must carry out her plan somehow. When Hamilton's life was completely wrecked, she would be ready to return to England - not till then; and she lay awake at nights grinding her long, narrow, wolf-like teeth together as she thought of Hamilton in the desert bungalow.

One morning, after a nearly sleepless night, she got up and looked critically at her face in the glass. Old and haggard as usual it looked; but to-day, in addition to age and care, a specially evil determination sat upon it.

"Life is practically done with," she thought, looking at it. "I have only this one thing to care about now, and I'll do it somehow before I go. If I can't enjoy my life, he shan't enjoy his."

She turned from the glass, and commenced dressing. The evil look deepened on her face from minute to minute, and the word "Beast!" came at intervals through her teeth.

Outside the window of her charming room all was waking in the joyous dawn of the East. Long shadows lay across the velvet green slopes of the Commissioner's lawn as the sun rose behind the majestic palms that shaded it; floods of golden light were rippling softly over roses and stephanotis, opening bud after bud to the azure above women; the gay call of the birds rang through the clear morning air; the perroquets swung in ecstasy on the bamboo branches, crying out shrill comments on each other's toilet. The scent of a thousand blossoms rose up like some magic influence, stealing through the sparkling sunlight into the room, and played round the thin face of the woman within, but it could make no message clear to her. Every sense of hers had long been sealed to all joy by hate.

At breakfast she announced her intention of leaving India by the following mail, and not all the kind pressure brought to bear upon her by the Commissioner's wife could induce her to postpone her departure. She was gentle, calm, and resigned in manner, as usual, excessively grateful for all they had done for her, and the kindness shown her. She spoke very sweetly of her husband, told them how she had hoped by coming out to induce him to leave the evil life he was leading; but she saw now that these things lay in higher hands than hers, and she felt all she could do was to pray and hope for him in silence.

"Why don't you divorce him?" broke in the Commissioner abruptly and quickly, anxious to get it out before his wife could stop him. He tugged violently at his moustache, waiting for her answer. If she would do that, he was thinking, what a relief for that poor devil Hamilton!

"Divorce him?" returned Mrs. Hamilton resignedly. "Never! It is a wife's duty to submit to whatever cross Providence lays upon her, but divorce seems to me only the resource of abandoned women."

The Commissioner's wife nodded her head in majestic

approval. The Commissioner got up abruptly, breakfast being concluded. He said nothing, but his mental ejaculation was, "Old hag! knows she couldn't get any one else, nor half such a handsome allowance!"

The day for Mrs. Hamilton's departure came, and on its morning Hamilton found a note from her on his office desk. He took it up and opened it with a feeling of repulsion.

"DEAR FRANK, - I am leaving by the noon boat for England. They seem to have altered their time of sailing to twelve instead of seven P.M.

> "I am sorry my visit here has caused you trouble. Do not be too hard on me. I am leaving now, and do not intend to worry you again. You must lead your own life until, perhaps, some day you wish to return to me. You will find me ready to welcome you. Good-bye, and forgive any pain I have caused you. - Your affectionate wife,
>
> JANE."

Hamilton read this note with amazement, and a sense of its falsity swept over him, as if a wind had risen from the paper and struck his face. But as men too often do, he tried to thrust away his first true instincts, and replace their warning with a lumbering reason. He sat deep in thought, gazing at the table before him. If it were true, if she were really going, if she really meant good-bye, what a relief! But it was impossible, unless, indeed, she had accomplished her plan, and had heard that he had been, or was about to be dismissed from his post.

This seemed to throw a light upon the matter, and with the idea of finding confirmation of this in some of the other letters awaiting him, he started to go through them. It was a heavy post-bag, and gave him much to attend to. He went through the letters, but found nothing relative to himself in them, and settled down to his work. Twelve, one, and two passed, and he looked up at the clock, wondering if she were really gone. He seemed to have no inclination for lunch, so he worked on without leaving the office, and only rose to clear his desk when it was time to leave for the day. To-morrow he would learn definitely what passengers the out-going boat had carried. He would not stay this evening to find out. He felt ill, listless; he only wanted to be back with Saidie in the restful shade of the palms.

As he rode across the desert that evening an indefinable depression hung over him. Never since he had found Saidie had that melancholy, once so natural, come back to him. Her spirit, whether she were absent or present, seemed always with him - a gay, bright, beautiful vision ever before his eyes, giving him the feeling that he was looking always into sunlight. But to-night there seemed emptiness, gloom about him.

"It's the weather," he muttered, and looked upward to the curious sky. It was gold, gleaming gold; but close to the horizon lay two bright purple bars, like lines of writing in the West: the prophecy of a storm, and the heat seemed to hang in the air that not a faintest breath moved.

Swiftly and evenly the great camel bore him, its well-beloved master, over the rippling sand towards the palms in the golden west, but the approaching night travelled faster than they, and it was quite dark, with a sullen heavy darkness, before they reached the bungalow. It seemed very quiet, with an indefinable sense of stillness in the garden and wide hall. Neither Saidie nor any servant came to meet him, and it was quite dark: no lamp had been lighted. With a sudden throb of terror in his heart, Hamilton paused and called "Saidie."

There was no response, no sound. Striking a match, Hamilton deliberately lit a lamp. Some great evil was upon him, and with a curious calmness he went forward to meet it. He went upstairs and pushed open the door of their bedroom, shielding the light with his hand and seeking first with his eyes the bed. Saidie lay there: the exquisite form, in its transparent purple gauze, lay composed upon the bed, a little to one side. The glorious hair, unbound, rippled in a dark river to the floor; the head rested sideways as in sleep, upon the pillow. In silence Hamilton approached; near the bed his foot slid suddenly; he looked down; there was a tiny lake of scarlet blood, blackening at its edges, blood on the wooden bedstead side, blood on the purple muslin over the perfect breasts. Hamilton, his body growing rigid, put out his hand to her forehead; it was cold. He set down the lamp and turned her face towards it, putting his arm under her head. Her lips were stone colour, the lids were closed over the eyes; the face was the face of death.

In those moments Hamilton realized that his own life was over. Saidie was dead - murdered. The world then was simply no more for him. All was finished: he himself was a dead man. Only one thing remained, one duty for him. To avenge her! Then utter rest and blackness. He looked round thinking. The room was quite empty, undisturbed. The great pearls on Saidie's neck were untouched. They gleamed gently in the pale light from his lamp. No robber, no outsider had been here. Then, in the darkened room, leapt up before him the truth: a white, blonde face seemed looking at him from the walls - the thick pale lips, the half-closed sinister eyes, the lean long figure of his wife rose before him.

"But she was to leave by the morning's boat," he muttered. Then ... a thought struck him. He withdrew his arm gently from the passive head, lighted another lamp, putting it on a bracket in the wall, and left the room, descending to the vacant hall. He went to the verandah and called to his servants. They came, a trembling crowd, with upraised hands, and fell flat before him, weeping and striking their heads on the ground.

"It is not our fault, Light of Heaven, Father of the Poor, the Mem-Sahib came - the white Mem-Sahib. We are poor men; we have no fault at all."

Hamilton listened for a moment to the storm of words and protesting cries. Then he raised his hand and there was silence, but for a sound of rising wind without and the sobbing of the natives.

Victoria Cross

"Pir Bakhs," he said to the head of them all, the butler, "tell me all you know. Your mistress is dead. Who is responsible?"

The butler came forward and fell at his master's feet with clasped hands.

"Lord of the Earth, I know nothing but this. At five all was quiet in the house, and our mistress sat in the garden singing. Then came to the door two runners with a palanquin. They asked to see our mistress. I said wait. I went to the garden. I said the white Mem-Sahib has come in a palanquin. My mistress said, 'I will see her.' She went to the drawing-room, and the white Mem-Sahib came in, and they drank tea together. Your servant is a poor man, and he saw no more till the runners went away with the palanquin. So we said, 'The white Mem-Sahib has gone,' and my mistress said to me she felt drowsy and must sleep, and went upstairs to the Light of Heaven's room and shut the door. And your servant was laying the table in your honour's dining-room a little later, and he went to close the jillmills,[1] for the wind was rising, and your servant saw through the jillmill the white Mem-Sahib again getting into her palanquin that had appeared once more at the back, and the runners ran with it very fast into the desert; then your servant ran out to ask the other servants why the white Mem-Sahib had come back, and the ayah met him at the door and said she had found our mistress killed in her room; and your honour's servant is a poor man, and has wept ever since."

[Footnote 1: Wooden shutters.]

Hamilton listened in perfect silence. The man's face was lined with grief, the tears rolled in streams down his livid cheeks. A wail went up from the other servants at his words. Hamilton and his mistress were their idols, and his grief was very real to themselves.

Hamilton stretched out his hand to the trembling man with a benign gesture.

"Pir Bakhs, I believe you. You have served me many years, and never lied to me. This is another's work, not yours. Be at peace. You have no fault."

The butler wept louder, and the others wailed with him, calling upon Heaven to bless their master and avenge their mistress.

Hamilton turned from them to the dark dining-room, which he crossed to the hall; through this he walked in the darkness as a blind man walks, to the entrance.

He tore the wood-work door open, wrenching it from its hinges, and looked out into the night. A dust-storm was raging in the desert beyond the compound, and its stinging blasts of wind, laden with sand, drove heavily over the exquisite masses of bloom, the glorious and delicate scented blossoms of the garden. It tore off the flowers remorselessly, and even for the moment he stood there, a rain of thin, white, shredded petals was flung into his face. The branches of the trees groaned and whined in the thick darkness, the swish of broken and bent bamboo came from all sides, the roar of the dust driven through the foliage filled his ears. The garden, the beautiful, sheltered garden, scene of their delights, was being ruthlessly destroyed, even as his life had been; it was expiring in agony, even as he would shortly expire: to-morrow it would be desolate, a shattered wreck under the dust, even as he, in a little while - But something should be done first.

Leaving the doorway open, letting the dust-laden wind tear shrieking through the silent house, he plunged into the roaring darkness. He took the centre path that led straight to the compound gate. The unhappy bushes and tortured branches of the trees, bent and twisted by the onrushing wind, lashed his face and body as he went down the path. He did not feel their stinging blows. On, on to the desert he went blindly but steadily in the thick darkness.

When he got beyond the compound gate, out of the shelter of

the garden, the weight of the wind almost bore him down; but as he faced its blast, his eyes saw, not so very far, out on the plain, dull in the whirling mist, the dancing uncertain light of a carried lantern. As the tiger darts forward on its prey, as the snake springs to the attack, Hamilton leapt forward into the wall of wind that faced him and ran at the dancing light.

Choked with sand, blinded, suffocated and breathless, but full of power to kill, he was on it at last, and flung himself with sinewy hands on the swaying, covered sedan chair, between the two bearers, who, bewildered and helpless in the sudden storm, were groping slowly across the plain. With a shriek they dropped the handles, as Hamilton flung himself suddenly on the chair; the lantern fell into the sand and went out. The natives, thinking the devil, the actual spirit of the storm, had overtaken them, fled howling into the blackness, their cries swallowed up like whispers in the roar of the wind. As the chair struck the sand, the woman within thrust her head with a cry through the open side. Hamilton seized it by the neck. Out! out of the sedan chair, through the burst-open door, he pulled the wretched creature by her head, and then flung her with all his force upon the sand.

The raging wind swept past them in sheets of dust, bellowing as it went. He knelt on her body; his hands ground into her neck. Through the darkness he saw beneath him the thin, white oval of the face, with its eyes bulging, starting out of the head, its lips writhing in agony; two white hands beat helplessly in the black air beside him. He looked hard into her eyes, bending down to her close, very near, as his hands sank deeper into her neck, his fingers locked more tightly round it. In a few seconds the light of the eyes went out, the hands ceased to beat the air. Saidie was avenged. With a laugh that rang out into the noise of the storm, the man got up from the limp body and stood by it, in the echoing darkness. Then he kicked it, so that it rolled over, and the sand came up in waves eager to bury it.

In an hour woman, sedan chair, lantern would all be beneath a level plain of sand.

He turned back towards the bungalow. "Saidie," he murmured, and the storm-wind seemed to rave "Saidie!" "Saidie!" round him, to whirl the name upwards to the dim stars, glimmering one here and there, far off and veiled in the heavens. He went back; the wind helped him. On its wings he seemed borne back to his house, through the tortured garden, through the gaping doorway, over the shattered door he passed, and then up the stairs to their room.

After the inferno of the desert the inside of the house seemed quiet, and in their room the lamps burned steadily, but low. Their oil was used up, their life, like his, was nearly done. The bed stood there and on its calm white stillness lay Saidie, waiting for him, for him alone, as always.

He went up to her and stood there.

"Saidie?" but she did not answer. He lay down beside her gently, so as not to break her slumber, and then drew her to his breast. Ah his treasure! his world! Surely now all was well since she was safe in his arms! He did not feel the deathly coldness. There was a whizzing in his brain where Nature had laid her finger on a vein, and broken it that he might be released from sorrow and die.

"Saidie?" he murmured again as her breast pressed his, and put his lips to hers.

As his life had first dawned in her kiss, so it went back now to the lips that had given it, and in that kiss he died.

II

There was complete silence in the large room, filled with long, wavering shadows that the flickering firelight chased over the walls and amongst the gilt-edged tables.

Beyond the windows the dusk was gathering quickly in the wind-swept street, beneath the leaden sky. From the pane nearest the fire a side-light fell across a man's figure leaning against the corner of the mantel-shelf. A ruddy glow from the hearth struck upon the silk skirt of a girl leaning back in the easy-chair beneath the other corner.

Her face is lost in the shadow.

He is a good-looking fellow, very. The high white collar that shows up in the dusk is fastened round a long, well-set neck; the figure in the blue serge suit is straight and pleasing, and the shoulders erect and slim.

The girl's eyes, looking out of the shadow, take in these points, and the pleasure they give her seems inextricably confused with dull pain. Her gaze passes on to his face, and rests eagerly, almost thirstily, upon it.

There is light enough still to show her its well-cut oval, spoiled now by the haggard falling in of the cheeks, the lines in the forehead, and the swellings beneath the eyes.

He shifts his position a little and glances through the window.

His eyes are full of irritation, and the girl knows it, though they are turned from her. She gives a suppressed, inaudible sigh; his attitude now brings out the impatient discontent on his mouth and the rigid determination of the chin.

"I suppose you mean two people can live upon nothing?" His voice is cold, even hostile, and he speaks apparently to the panes, but the tones are well-bred and pleasing; and again the girl wonders dimly which is the predominating sensation in her - pleasure or pain.

"No," she says, in rather a suffocated voice. "But I say, if either person has enough, or the two together, it does not matter which has it, or which has the most."

Silence, which her hesitating, timid voice breaks at last.

"Does it?"

"Yes, I think it does," he answered shortly. "The man must have enough to support both, or he has no right to marry at all."

The girl's hands lock themselves together convulsively, unseen behind her slight waist, laced so skilfully into the fashionable bodice.

There is a hard decision in the incisive tones that does not belong to the mere expression of a general theory - a cold authority and a weight of personal conviction that turns the words into a statement of rigid principle.

The girl feels almost dizzy, and she closes her hot eyelids suddenly to shut out the line of that hard, obstinate chin.

"People's ideas on what is enough to support both vary so much," she says quietly, with well-bred indifference in her tone, while her heart beats wildly as she waits for his next remark.

"Well, what would you consider enough yourself?" he says coldly, after a slight pause, turning a little more towards her.

The red light glows steadily on her skirts, and he can see the graceful outline of her knees under them, and one small foot upon the hearthrug; the rest of the form is veiled in the shadow, except one rounded line of a shoulder and the glint of light hair above.

He looks down at her, and there seems a sudden, nervous expansion in his frame; outwardly there is not the faintest impatient movement. He waits quietly for her reply.

The girl hesitates as she looks at him. To her, in her absorbing love for the man before her, the question is an absurd mockery.

To reduce to a certain number of pounds this "enough," when for her anything or nothing would be enough!

"I would rather starve to death in your arms than live another day without you," is the current running under all her thoughts, and it confuses them and makes it difficult for her to speak.

What shall she answer? To name a sum too small in his eyes will be as great an error as to name one too large. He would only think her a silly, sentimental girl, who knows nothing of what she is talking about, and who has no knowledge and appreciation of the responsibilities of life.

Besides, to name a very small income will be to conjure up before his eyes the picture of a mean, pitiful, sordid existence, from which she feels, with painful distinctness, he would turn with disgust.

Poor? Yes, he has told her that he is poor, and she believes it; but somehow - by contracting debt, probably - she thinks, as her keen, observant eyes sweep over him, he manages at present to live and dress as a gentleman.

Those well-cut suits, those patent shoes and expensive cigarettes; these things, she feels instinctively, must be preserved for him, or any form of life would lose its charm.

At the same time, she must mention something that is not hopelessly beyond him. She recalls her own two hundred; surely, at the least, he must be making one.

"I can hardly say," she murmured at last, "because personally I think one can live on so very little; but I suppose most people would say - well, about three hundred pounds a year."

"Oh! three hundred a year," he says, stretching out his hand for the tea-cup on a low table beside him. The tea has grown cold in the discussion of abstract questions. He takes the cup and sits down deliberately in the corner of the couch opposite her, and stirs the tea slowly.

"How much is that a week? Five pounds fifteen, isn't it? Well, now, go on, see what you can make of it. Your house - the smallest - and servants -"

"House and servants!" interrupts the girl, "but why have a house and servants at all?"

"I don't know," he rejoins curtly, "because the girl generally expects those things when she marries."

"Not all girls," she says, and one seems to hear the smile with which she says it in her voice.

"You mean rooms?" he says quickly, with a gleam of pleasure breaking for a moment across his face.

"Well - say rooms - you would want three - thirty shillings, I suppose, at the least, and then another thirty for board. That leaves two fifteen for everything else."

"Surely that's a good deal."

"Oh, I don't know; think of one's clothes," and Stephen stares moodily into the fire, with a pricking recollection of a tailor's bill for twenty odd in his drawer at home now.

Then, to remove the impression of selfish extravagance he feels he may have given, he adds:

"And a man wants to give his wife some amusement, and three hundred a year leaves nothing for that."

"Amusement!" the girl repeats, starting up and standing upright, with one elbow just touching the mantelpiece, and the firelight flooding her figure from the slim waist downwards. "What amusement does a woman want if she is in love with the man she is living with? The man himself is her amusement! To watch him when he is occupied, to wait for him when he is away, to nurse him when he is ill - that is her amusement: she does not want any other!"

Stephen stares at the flexible form, and listens to the words that he would admire, only the cynical suspicion is in his mind that she is talking for effect. His general habit was to consider all women mercenary and untrustworthy. Deep in his heart - for he had a heart, though contracted from want of use - lay a hungry desire to be loved, really loved for himself; and the very keenness of the longing, and the anxiety not to be deceived, lessened his powers of penetration, and blinded him to the girl's character.

He laughs slightly. "You are taking a theatrical view of the whole thing!"

"How do you mean?"

"Oh, well, that the wife really loves her husband and sticks to him through everything, and they pass through unheard-of difficulties together, and so on"; but he adds, with a faint yawn: "I've always noticed that when the money goes the love disappears too. There's no love where there's abject poverty."

"But three hundred a year is not abject poverty," answers the girl in a quiet tone, not denying his theory for fear of being called again theatrical.

"No," he admits. "Oh, it might do very well as long as there were only two; but then, when there are children, it means a nurse, and all sorts of expenses."

He says the words with a simplicity and directness that makes the girl almost catch her breath. For these two were not on intimate terms with each other, not even terms of intimate speaking.

Nothing had passed between them yet but the merest society phrases, and before a certain quiet dinner one month back neither knew of the other's existence. Since then some chance meetings on the beach, the parade, the pier, a few long afternoon rows, between then and now: these are the only nourishment the flame in either breast has received - a flame kindled in a few long glances across the dinner-table.

But this afternoon he has laid aside the customary phrases and deliberately commenced the present conversation.

True, it is purely an abstract one - all theory and hypotheses. No one could say otherwise if it were repeated. Not a personal word has been uttered on either side; but the girl feels in the determined tone of his voice, in the studied way he started it, in the cold precision with which he follows it, that it is practically a test conversation of herself, and that she is virtually passing through an examination.

He has come this afternoon with a set of certain questions that he means to put, to all of which her answers are received without comment, and mentally noted down.

He neither repeats himself, nor presses a point, nor leaves out anything on his mental list, nor allows any remark to lead away from it.

He has also certain things he means to say, which he will say, as he asks his questions, deliberately, one after the other; and then, when he has heard and said all he intends, he will terminate the conversation as decisively as he began it and go. The girl feels all this, for her brain is as clear and keen as the glance of her eyes.

She knows that he is testing her: that she stands upon trial before him.

She has nothing to hide: only, that too great love and devotion, that seems to swell and swell irrepressibly within her, and would pour itself out in words to him, but that his tone, his manner, his look keep it back absolutely, as a firm hand holds down the rising cork upon the exuberant wine. And now, at this sentence of his, her words fail her. They are strangers practically, that is conventionally - quite strangers, she remembers confusedly - but for this secret bond of passion, knit up between them, which both can feel but both ignore.

The natural male in him, and the natural female in her, are already, as it were, familiar, but the fashionable man and girl are strangers still.

Then, now, how is she to say what she wishes to him? How can she talk with this mere acquaintance upon this subject? The very word "children" seems to scorch her lips. At the same time, familiarity with him seems natural and unnatural; terrible, and yet simple.

Then, too, what are his views?

Will her next words shock him inexpressibly?

In her passionate, excitable brain, inflamed with love for the man, the idea of maternity can merely present itself like an unwelcome, grey-clad Quaker at a banquet.

She hesitates, choosing her words. She knows so little of the man in front of her. His clothes, she sees, are of the newest cut, but his notions may not be.

At last her soft, weak, timid voice breaks the pause.

"Do you think it necessary to have very large families?"

"No, I don't," he answers instantly with the energy and alacrity of one who is glad to express his opinion. "No, I don't, not at all."

The girl's suspended breath is drawn again. Unlike himself in his queries she presses her point home.

"Don't you think those marriages are the happiest where there are no children?"

"Yes," he says decidedly, getting up and thrusting his hands into his coat pockets. "Yes, I do - much the happiest."

There is silence. It is too dark for either to see the other's expression. He stands irresolutely for a minute or two, and then says with a disagreeable laugh:

"I should hate my own children! Fancy coming home and finding a lot of children crying and screaming in the place."

To this the girl says nothing, and Stephen, after a minute's reflection, softens his words.

"Besides, your wife's love, when she has children, is all given to them."

"Yes," murmurs her well-bred voice. "Oh, yes, one is happier without them."

Neither speak. They are agreed so far; there is a deep relief and pleasure in the breast of each.

"Well," he says at last, rousing himself, "I must go. I shall be late for dinner."

The girl leans down and stirs the fire into a leaping, yellow blaze. It fills the room with light, and reveals them fully now to each other.

She makes no effort to detain him, and they look at each other, about to part.

The self-control of each is marvellous, and admirable for its mere thoroughness and completeness.

He has large eyes, and they stare down at her haggardly, as he stands facing her in the light. The hungry, hopeless look in those eyes and the drawn lines in his face go to the girl's heart, and to herself it seems literally melting into one warm flood of sympathy.

Ill! he looks ill and wretched, and she longs with a longing that presses upon her, till it is like a physical agony, to give some way to her feelings.

"Dearest, my dearest!" she is thinking, "if I might only tell you - even a little -"

And Stephen stares at the soft face and warm lips, half-paralyzed with desire to bend down and kiss them. How would a kiss be? How would they - And so there is a momentary, barely perceptible pause, filled with a painful intensity of feeling, to which neither gives way one hair's breadth. Then he gives a curt laugh.

"We have discussed rather a difficult problem and not settled it," he says in a conventional tone.

"It seems to me quite simple," murmurs the girl, with a throat so dry that the words are hardly audible.

He hears, but makes no reply beyond another slight laugh, as he holds out his hand. The girl puts hers into it. There is a moderate pressure only on either side, and then he goes out and shuts the door, leaving the girl standing motionless - all the warm springs in her heart frozen by his last cynical laugh.

Brookes finds his way down the stairs, through the unlighted hall, and lets himself out in the chill October air.

He goes down the street feeling a confused sense of having inflicted pain and left distress behind him, but his own sensation of irritation, his own vexation and angry resentment against his lot in life, all but obliterate it.

For some seconds he walks on with all his thoughts merged together in a mere desperate and painful confusion. "Only a hundred a year!" is his plainest, most bitter reflection. "Five-and-twenty, and only earning a hundred a year!"

Brookes is not of a calm temperament. His nervous system is tensely strung, and generally, owing to various incidental matters, slightly out of tune, or at anyrate, feels so.

His circulation is rapid, every pulse beats strongly, and the blood flows hotly in his veins.

His mental nature is of much the same order - passionate, excitable, and impatient; but there is such a heavy curb-rein of control perpetually upon it, that its three leading qualities jar inwardly upon himself more than they show to outsiders.

Even now the confused, excited disorder in his brain is soon regulated and calmed by his will, and as he walks on he lapses into trying to recollect whether he has said all he meant to.

He concludes that he has, and a certain satisfaction comes

over him.

"Well, I have told her my views now," he reflects. "She sees what I think, and what my principles are. She won't wonder that I say nothing. I shall try for another post and a rise of salary, and then -"

Stephen's character was a fine one in its way. The capacity for self-command and self-denial was tremendous, his sense of honour keen, his adherence to that which he conceived the right inflexible, his will immutable; but of the subtler sweetness of the human heart he had none.

Of sympathy, the divine [Greek: sym, pathos], *the suffering with*, he had not the vaguest conception: of its faint and poor reflections, pity and mercy, he had but a dim idea.

He stuck as well as he could to what he thought was the right path, and as to the feelings of others, he could not be blamed for not considering them, for he had never practically realized that they had any.

In the present circumstances he had a few, fine, adamantine rules for conduct, which he was going to steadfastly apply, and he thought no more of the girl's feelings under them than one thinks of the inanimate parcel one is cording with what one knows is good, stout string.

In his eyes it was distinctly dishonourable for a man to engage a girl to himself without a reasonably near prospect of marriage.

It was also decidedly ungentlemanly to propose to a girl if she had money and you had none. Moreover, it was extremely selfish to remove a girl from a comfortable position to a poorer one, though she might positively swear she preferred it; and lastly, it was unwise for various reasons, to be too amiable to the girl, or to give any but the dimmest clue to your own feelings.

There was no telling - your feelings might change even - when you have to wait so long - and then it was much better, *for the girl*, that she should not be tied to you.

To visit the girl frequently, to hang about her to the amusement of onlookers, to keep alive her passion by look and hint and innuendo, to excite her by advances when he was in the humour, and studiously repulse her when she made any, to act almost as if he were her *fiance*, and curtly resent it if she ever assumed he was more than an ordinary friend - this line of action he saw no fault in. The above were his views, and they were excellent, and if the girl didn't understand them she might do the other thing.

Some weeks passed, and the man and the girl saw each other constantly - three or four times in the week, perhaps more; and the inward irritation grew intense, while their outward relations remained unchanged.

There was a certain brutality that crept into the man's tones occasionally when he addressed her, a certain savage irritability in manner, that told the girl's keen intelligence something; some involuntary sighs of hers as she sat near him, and an increasing look of exhaustion on her face, that told him something. But that was all.

There were no tender passages between them; none of the conventional English flirting - matters were too serious, and the nature of each too violent to permit of that. A little bitter, more or less hostile, conversation passed between them on the most trifling subjects in his long afternoon calls. A little music would be attempted - that is, he would sing song after song, while she accompanied him, but a song was rarely completed. Generally, before or at the middle, he would seize the music in a gust of irrepressible and barely-veiled irritability, and fling it on the piano - yet they attempted the music with unwavering persistence, and both rose to go to the instrument with mutual alacrity.

There they were close to each other - so close that the warmth and breath of their beings were interchanged. There in the pursuit of a fallen sheet of music, his head bent down and touched hers. Once, apparently to regain the leaf, his hand and arm leaned hard upon her lap. One second, perhaps, no more; but the girl's whole strained system seemed breaking up at the touch - her control shattered, like machinery violently reversed.

The music leaf was replaced, but her hands had fallen nerveless from the keys.

"It is hot. I can't go on playing. Put the window open, will you, for me?"

Stephen walked to the window, raised it, and smiled into the dark.

That night it seemed to Stephen he could never force himself to leave the girl. He prolonged the playing past all reasonable limits, until May's sister laughingly reminded him that they were only staying in seaside lodgings, and other occupants of the house must be considered. Stephen reluctantly relinquished the friendly piano, and then stood, with May's sweet figure beside him, and her upraised face clear to the side vision of his eye, talking to her sister.

At last, when every trifle is exhausted of which he can make conversation, there comes a pause, a silence; he can think of nothing more. He nerves himself, holds out his hand, and says, "Good-night!"

May, influenced equally by the same indomitable aversion to be separated from him, follows him outside the drawing-room, and another pause is made on the stair. By this time a fresh stock of chaff and light wit is ready in Stephen's brain, and he makes use of anything and everything to procure him another moment at her side; but of all the passion within him, of the ardent, impetuous impulse towards her, nothing, not the faintest trace, shows.

A mere "Good-night!" ends their conversation at length, and the girl did not re-enter the drawing-room, but passed straight up the stairs to her own room.

"Does he care? Does he care or not?" she asked herself, walking ceaselessly backwards and forwards. "If I only knew that he did! This is killing me; and suppose, after all, he does not care!"

She almost reels in her walk, and then stretches her arms out on her mantelpiece, and leans her head heavily upon them.

"So this is being in love!" she thinks, with a faint satirical smile. "All this anxiety and pain and feeling of illness! Why, it is as if poison had been poured through me."

Through the next day May lay pallid and silent on the couch, without pretence of occupation, feeling too exhausted even to respond to her sister's chaff and raillery.

It was only at dinner, when her brother-in-law informed his wife he was sick of the place, and that nothing would induce him to stay more than another week, that a stain of scarlet colour appeared in May's cheeks and a terrified dilation in her eyes.

Her lids were lowered directly, and the blood receded again. She made no remark, but at the close of dinner she excused herself, and went upstairs alone.

Once in her room, she stripped off her dinner-dress and shoes, and re-dressed in morning things. Her hands trembled so violently that she could hardly fasten her bodice over the wildly-expanding bosom.

But her resolve was fixed. They were going in a week. To-morrow, she knew, Stephen was leaving the place for a fortnight. She must see him to-night.

When she is completely dressed, she pauses for a moment to choke down the terrible physical excitement that seems to rob her of breath and muscular power.

Then she passes downstairs quietly and goes out.

The night is still, cold, and dark.

May walks rapidly through the few streets that divide his house and hers.

The few men she meets turn involuntarily to glance after the splendid form that goes by them, and in her decisive walk, in the eyes blind to them, they feel instinctively she is already owned, mentally or actually, by some one other.

When she reaches Stephen's house, she learns he is in, and with a great fear of him suddenly rushing over her, she sends word up to him by the servant: Will he see her?

While she waits in the hall, her message is taken upstairs. May leans against the wall, a terrible sick faintness, born of excitement and hysteria, coming suddenly upon her.

There is a hall-chair, but her eyes are too darkened to see it; she simply clings to the handle of the door, and lets her head sink against the side of the passage.

Brookes is upstairs with his brother and two friends; they have been playing cards, but a game is just over, and the men have got up to stretch themselves.

Stephen himself is leaning back against the mantelpiece, as his habit is, and yawning slightly. He has just been beaten, and he is a man who can't play a losing game.

"No," his brother remarks. "I didn't know what the deuce

'Ladas' meant till I looked it up; did you, Steve?"

"Oh, I should think every schoolboy would know that," is the curt response, and at that moment the servant's knock comes at the door.

"Please, sir, there's a lady as wants to see you," the girl says with a perceptible grin. "She said she wouldn't come up, and she's waiting in the hall, sir."

There is a blank silence in the room. Brookes pales suddenly, and his eyebrows, that habitually have a supercilious elevation, rise still higher with annoyance.

He hesitates a single second, then, without a word in reply, he crosses the room towards the door, and the servant retreats hastily.

The men glance furtively at each other, but Stephen's devil of a temper being well known, they forbear to laugh or even smile till he is well out of the room. Brookes goes down the stairs with one sentence only in his mind: Coming to my rooms, and making a fool of me!

He is annoyed, intensely annoyed, and that is his sole feeling.

May is standing upright now in the centre of the hall under the swinging lamp, and she watches him run lightly down the long flight of stairs towards her with swimming eyes.

What is there in that figure of his that has so much influence on her senses? More, perhaps, even than his face, do the lines of his neck and shoulders and their carriage please her. All the pleasure she can ever realise in life seems contained for her in that slim, well-made frame, in its blue serge suit.

She makes one impetuous step forward, her whole form dominated, impelled by the surge of ardent feelings within her, and holds out one trembling, burning hand. Stephen, with a confused sense of its being awfully bad form that she should be standing in his hall, takes it in his right hand, feeling hastily for the lucifers with his left.

"Er - come into the dining-room, won't you?" he says, with the familiar, supercilious accent that with him is the expression of suppressed annoyance and slight embarrassment.

He knows the rooms are unlet, and with gratitude for this providential circumstance in his thoughts, and his heart beating violently with sudden excitement now he is actually in her presence, he turns the handle of the door and sets it wide open.

He strikes a match and holds it up, leaning back against the door, for her to pass in before him.

As she does so, their two figures for one second almost touch each other, and a sudden glow lights up in his veins. He feels it, and it warns him instantly to summon his self-control. That before everything.

The next moment he follows her into the room, lights the gas, returns to the door, closes it, and then comes back towards the rug where she is standing.

By this time his command is his own. His face is as calm as a mask. His large eyes, somewhat bloodshot now from hours of smoking and a sleepless night, rest upon her with cold enquiry.

She has seen them once, met them once, fixed, liquid, with passionate longing upon hers; desperately she seeks in them now for one gleam of the same light, but there is none. They and his face are cloaked in a cold reserve. Sick, and with her heart beating to suffocation, she says, as he waits for her to explain her presence:

"We are - going away."

Stephen's heart seems to contract at the words he had so often dreaded to hear, heard at last.

His thoughts take a greyer hopelessness.

"Oh, really!" he says merely, the shock he feels only slightly intensifying his habitual drawl. "Not immediately, I hope?"

Nothing to the nervous, excited, over-strained girl before him could be more galling, more humiliating, more crushing than the cold, conventional politeness of his tones and words.

This frightful fence of Society manner that he will put between them - a slight, delicate defence, is as effectual as if he caused a precipice by magic to yawn between them.

"No - not - not - quite immediately, but soon," she falters. "And it seems as if I could not exist if - I - never see you."

There is a strained pause while they stand facing each other. He is motionless; one hand rests in his pocket, the other hangs nerveless at his side.

They look at each other. Each is thinking of the supreme delight - even if momentary - the other's embrace could give if - but the conditions in the respective minds are different - in his: "If I thought it wise;" in hers: "If he only would."

"Well, we can write to each other," he says at last.

"Oh, but what are letters?" the girl says passionately; and then, urged on hard by her love for him, her intuition of his love for her, and her common-sense instinct not to throw away her life's happiness for a misunderstanding or petty feeling of pride, she adds: "You know - don't you? - that I care for you more than anything else in the world."

Her tones are sharp with the intensity of feeling, and she stretches both hands imploringly a little way towards him.

He sees them quiver and her face whiten, and the frightened appeal increase in her pained eyes searching his face, and it is a marvel - later, he marvels at it himself - how, with his own passion keen and alive in him, he maintains his ground. But there is something in the whole scene that jars upon him - something theatrical that makes the thought flash upon him: Is it a got-up thing?

This puts him on the defensive directly; besides, he resents her coming to him in this way, and endeavouring to surprise from him words he has already explained to her he is unwilling to say.

She is trying to rush him, he puts it to himself; and the thought rouses all his own obstinacy and self-will.

When he chooses he will speak, and not before.

"It is very good of you to say so," he answers quietly, in a cold formal tone, and the girl quivers as if he had struck her.

Now, in his lonely, sleepless nights, the misery on the white face comes back and back to him in the darkness of his room, but then he is blind to it.

In an annoyed mood to begin with, irritated beyond bearing by his own helpless, ignominious position, as he fancies, he has no perception left for his own danger of losing her.

And the man, who had lived till five-and-twenty, desiring real love, and not knowing it, deliberately trampled upon it without recognising what he did.

His words cut the girl terribly.

It seems impossible for the second that she can force herself to speak again to him, but the terrible, irrepressible longing within her nerves her for one more effort.

"Is that all you can tell me? Do you not care for me at all?"

He looks at her and hesitates. So modest, so appealing, so timid, and yet so passionate! Surely this is genuine love for him. Why thrust it back? But the thought recurs. No. She is rushing him; and he declines to be rushed. Also a sort of half-embarrassment comes over him, a nervous instinct to put off, ward off a scene in which he will be called upon to demonstrate feelings he may not satisfy.

He laughs slightly, and says:

"Of course I do! I like you very much!"

The tones are slighting and contemptuous, enough so to convey the polite warning: Don't go any further, and force me to be positively rude to you.

Swayed by his strong physical passion, and blinded by the dogged determination he has to remain master of it, he is absolutely insensible of another's suffering.

Had the girl had greater experience with men, more hardihood and less modesty; if she could have approached him, and taken his hands and pressed them to her bosom; if she had had the courage to force upon him the mysterious influence of physical contact, Stephen's control would have melted in the kindled fire.

Words stir the brain, and through the brain, the senses; but with
some people it's a long way round.

Touch stirs the nerves, and its flame runs through the body like a flying pain.

Stephen's physical nerves were far more sensitive than his brain, and had the girl been a woman of the half-world, or even of the world, she could have succeeded. But she was a girl; and her modesty and innocence, the chastity of all her mental and physical being, hung like dead weights upon her in the encounter.

His words, his tones, his glance simply paralyze her - not figuratively, but positively. Her physical power to move towards him, to make a further appeal to him, is gone. Speech is dried upon her lips, wiped from them as a handkerchief passed over them might take their moisture.

She looks at him, dumb, frenzied with the intense longing to throw herself actually at his feet, but yet held back by some irresistible power she cannot comprehend, any more than one can comprehend the stifling, overpowering force in a nightmare.

It is the simple result of her life, her breeding, her virtue, her character, her habits of control and reserve. She is the fashionable, well-brought-up girl, with all her sensitive instincts in revolt against forcing herself upon a man indifferent to her, and full of an overwhelming instinctive timidity that her desire is wild to break down and cannot.

She stares at him, lost in a sense of bitter pain. All her vigorous life seems wrung with pain, and in that torture, in which every nerve seems bruised and quivering, a faint smile twists at last the pale, trembling lips. "You would have made a good vivisector!" she says. Then, before he has time to answer, she turns the handle of the door behind her, opens it and goes out.

A second after the street door closes, and Stephen stands on the dining-room mat, looking down the empty hall. Thoroughly disturbed and excited, with all his own passion surging heavily through his blood, and her last sentence - that he does not understand any more than he understands his own cruelty - ringing in his ears, he hesitates a minute, and then re-enters the dining-room, shuts to the door, and walks savagely up and down.

"Extraordinary girl!" he mutters. "What does she want? What can I do? She knows I can say nothing at present, when I'm going into the work-house myself! But what a splendid creature she is! Lots of 'go' in her. Well, I don't care. I'll have her one day; but there's no use making a lot of talk about it now."

May walked away from his doorstep, no longer a sane human being, responsible for its actions. The whole physical, nervous system, weakened by months of self-control, and night following night of sleeplessness, was hopelessly dislocated now.

The whole weight of her excited passion, flung back upon the sensitive brain, turned it from its balance. It had been a brilliant brain, and that very excitability that had lent its brilliance was fatal to it now.

The hopeless passion ran like a corroding poison through the inflammable tissue.

She had put the matter to the test, and found that truth of which the mere possibility had been torture. He had absolutely rejected her. "He could not care for me," she kept repeating, as the silent air round her seemed full of his cold, short laughs.

His passion for her was dead. It had existed, surely - those looks of his, the sudden violence of his touch when there was any excuse for the slightest contact with her - or had it all been some curious dream?

She could not tell now, but whether it had been or not, it was no longer. To her that seemed the only explanation of his words and tones. To the tender female nature the depth of brutality in the passion of the male - that is, in fact, the very sign of it - remains always an enigma.

After the scene just passed, it seemed to the girl impossible, ludicrous, to suppose that Stephen loved her.

She had already made great allowance for him. She had a large share of the gift of her sex - intuition; and she had understood more than many women would have done, but to-night he had gone beyond the limits of her imagination.

"No man would be so intensely unkind to a woman he cared for," she argued. "For nothing, when there is no need."

She was not an unreasonable, nor selfish, nor silly girl. Had Stephen told her he loved her, but that they must suppress their passion, that she must wait, she would have obeyed him, and waited months, years, gone down to her grave waiting, in patient fidelity to him. Her qualities of control were as fine as his, and her devotion to a man who loved her would have been limitless, but, acting according to his views, Stephen had taken some trouble to convince her he was not the man, and she was convinced.

And being convinced, the vision of her life without him seemed just then a dismal waste, impossible to face.

In most of the actions of the human being, the physical state of the person at the time is the principal factor, and May's whole physical frame, violently over-strained, craved for rest - rest that the excited brain could not give. Rest was the urgent demand pressed by the breaking nervous system, and from these two thoughts - rest, oblivion - grew the dangerous thought of Death.

"Sleep and forget! but I can't," she thought, "and if I do, there is the horrible awakening;" and again her fatigue suggested all the past sleepless nights, and the craving of the body urged the brain to find better means of satisfying it, in the same way as the appetite for food forces the brain to devise methods for procuring it.

She walked on in a straight line from Stephen's house, and the road happened to pass a post-office. May stopped and looked absently through its lighted, notice-covered panes.

"Send him a few lines," she thought; "because I am so stupid, I could not tell him enough, and then -"

She did not finish the sentence, but all beyond was blank peace. She went in, bought a letter-card, and wrote: -

> "I could have loved you devotedly, intensely, had you wished it, but you have made it clear to-night that you do not want love - at any rate, not mine. I have discovered that I have courage enough to die, but not to live without you. I am going to the sea now, and in an hour we shall be separated for ever. I shall know nothing and you will care nothing, so it seems a good arrangement. My last thought will be of you, my last desire for you, my last breath your name."

She fastened it with an untrembling hand, passed out of the office, posted it, and went straight down a side street to the parade.

The night was still, bound in a frosty silence. The temperature sank momentarily, and the icy grip intensified in the air. Overhead the sky was black, and glittered coldly with the winter stars. Beside and behind her and before her not a living creature's footstep broke the silence. The sea lay smooth, black, and motionless on her left, like some huge sleeping monster.

She walked on rapidly: a glorious, vigorous, living, youthful figure, full of that tremendous activity of brain and pulse and blood, so valuable when there is a use for it, so dangerous when thrown back upon itself.

"How I could have loved him, worshipped him, lived for him, had he but wanted me!" is the one instinctive cry of her whole nature.

At the first easy descent to the beach she turns from the parade, and goes down, passing without hesitation from the light down to the moist darkness of the beach. To get away into oblivion, to escape from this maddening sense of pain, to lose it, let it go from her like a garment in the black water, is her only impelling instinct.

She sees the glimmer of the water before her without a shudder. How much dearer and more inviting it seems to her tired eyes than her bed at home, where so many, many sleepless, anguished nights have been spent! Here - rest and sleep, with no awakening to a grey and barren to-morrow. The thought of Death is lost. Desire for the cessation of pain is keener at its height than even the desire for life.

She stumbles on the wet, black beach at the water's edge, and then finds where it is slipping like oil over the sand.

She walks forward, and the chill of the water rises round her ankles, then her knees, then her waist, and then she throws herself face forwards on it, as she once thought to fling herself on his breast.

In a half-drunken satisfaction she stretches her arms out in it and commences to swim towards the horizon. "Like his arms!" she thinks, as the water encircles her. "Like his lips!" she thinks, as it presses on her throat. "And as cold as his nature."

*   *   *   *   *

The following morning is calm and still - a perfect specimen of wintry beauty. A light frost covers the ground and sparkles on the trees.

There is a faint chill in the clear air, a tranquil calm on the gently rising and falling sea and in the lucid sky.

The sunlight falling on Stephen's bed and across his sleeping face shows a smile there, and his arm, lying on the coverlet - an arm thinned by constant fever and night-sweats - rests, in his thoughts, round her neck; that white neck so sweetly familiar in his dreams.

After a time he wakes and yawns, and turns his head heavily towards the window; and farther as the happy unconsciousness of sleep recedes from his face, and recollection and intelligence come back to it, more clearly show the haggard lines, traced all over it, of self-repression, seaming and marking it at five-and-twenty.

"Another day to be got through," he thinks merely, as Nature's most precious gift - the light - pours glowing through the panes.

When half-an-hour later he opens his door to take in his boots, he finds two letters with them, and at the sight of one his heart beats hard.

The other is in the girl's handwriting, and he lays it on his toilet-table, with the thought, "Asking me to go and see her, I suppose," and turns to the other with a mad impatience.

This is evidently the official letter with reference to his post - the post that means to him but this one thing: her possession.

He bursts it open, and in less than two seconds his eye takes in its news: he has the appointment.

The blood leaps over his face, and an exultant fire runs through his frame and along his veins.

He replaces the letter quietly in its cover with but the slightest tremor of his fingers.

Then he gets up from the bedside and stands in the middle of the room, looking through the sparkling panes.

"I have her!" he is thinking. "Yes, by God! at last I have her!"

The day is glorified; life is transfigured.

Through his whole body mounts that boundless exhilaration

of desire on the point of satisfaction. Not momentary desire, easily and recently awakened, but the long desire that has been goaded and baited to fury through weeks and months of repression, and tempered to a terrible acuteness in pain and suffering, like steel by flame.

And now triumph, and a delight beyond expression, bounds like an electrified pulse throughout all his strong, vigorous frame.

The lines seem to fade from his face, the mouth relaxes, and then he laughs, as he makes a step towards the window, flings it open, and leans out into the keen air.

"At last I can speak out decently. No one could think I cared for her money, or any of that rot now. How unexpected! - this morning! Now I can tell her I'm free, independent! I am glad I waited - it was much better. Far better, as I said, to be patient. Last night I almost - and now I'm very glad I didn't."

He draws his head back, and turns to the glass to shave with a light heart.

As he does so, he sees her letter again, and picks it up. "You darling!" he thinks, "I'll make you understand all now."

Some miles westward of the pier, some fathoms deep, out of reach of the quiet sunlight lying on the surface, tosses the girl's body, senseless and pulseless, with all the million possibilities of pleasure that filled those keen nerves and supple limbs gone out of them for ever, and Stephen draws out her despairing letter of eternal farewell, with a smile lighting up his handsome, pleasing face.

"Yes, it was much better to wait," he murmurs, "I don't approve of rushing things!"

III

CHAPTER I

It was morning on the Blue Nile. The turbulent blue river
rolled joyously between its banks, for it was high Nile, and a
swift, light breeze was blowing - the companion of the Dawn.
The vault of the sky seemed arched at a great height above the
earth, springing clearly, without any object to break the line
from the horizon of gold sand, and full of those white, filmy,
light-filled gleaming clouds that are one of the wonders and
glories of Upper Egypt and the Soudan. It was a morning and
a scene to make a man's heart rise high in his breast, and cry
out, as his eyes turned from the level-sanded desert floor,
through sunlit space, to the vaulted roof, "After all, the world
is a good house to live in."

Slowly the strong yellow sunlight poured over the plain, the
bank and the river, gilding every ripple; and, as the light grew,
hundreds of delicate shapes - the forms of the ibis and
flamingo and crane, and other river-fowl - became visible,
crowding down the dark banks, with flapping of white and
crimson wings, and stretching of legs, and opening of beaks,
rustling down, shaking their feathers, to bathe and drink of the
Blue River.

Wonderful light, and miraculous, gleaming, cloud-filled sky,
and wonderful birds preening their plumage and calling to
each other, and wonderful breeze-swept water, bluer than the
bluest depths of the Indian Ocean.

It was still so early that, in the whole stretch of rollicking, tumbling, buoyant waters between bank and bank, only one piece of river-craft could be seen. This pushed onward, cleaving through the little billows in the teeth of the morning breeze. It was a tiny naphtha launch - a horrid, fussy, smoking little thing, cutting through breeze and water, and diffusing a scent of oil and greased iron in the pure and radiant air. A white bird on the bank looked at it, and rose with a startled note of alarm, and a flight of lovely-salmon-coloured colleagues followed. The others merely looked up and paused, with their wings wide stretched, and then went on calmly with their toilets - they had seen it before.

In the launch, of which the whole centre was taken by the naphtha-stove - the engine by courtesy - sat a young Englishman, whose face had that frank, attractive look of one whose thoughts are kindly, well disposed to all the world; and at stem and stern stood, erect and silent, the white-clothed figure of a boy from the Soudan. Lithe, graceful forms supported long necks and straight-featured faces, black as if carved out of smooth ebony, and contrasting strangely with the white turbans of stiff linen twisted deftly into a high crest above the brows. Swiftly the little boat ran on for a mile or two against wind, with its three silent and motionless occupants; then one boy turned, and pronounced solemnly the two words, "Mister, Omdurman!"

This was accompanied with a gracious wave of his hand towards the bank, as he leant forward to stop the engine, and his companion turned the boat to land.

Omdurman, as seen from the river level, looks like nothing but a long streak of duller yellow on the real gold of the African sand. Its tiny, square, flat-roofed mud-houses are not, with few exceptions, higher than six feet, and there is nothing else save them and their dreary, yellow-brown, muddy monotony in the whole village: not a palm, not a flower, not one blade of grass, simply a collection of low mud-houses, with trampled mud-paths between, and here and there an open, brown, dusty square.

The stillness and heat of the day were settling down now: the first wild, cool youth of the morning was past, and the Englishman felt the heat of the desert rise from the ground and strike his face, like the blow of a flail, as he stepped on land. He expected the Soudanese boys to follow, as they generally did on similar excursions - one to secure the boat and sit and wait beside it, and the other to accompany himself, carry his tripod and camera, and act as guide and general escort. To-day the boy stood in the boat, and addressed him earnestly:

"Boat wanted by other misters: let us go back: take them. We make much money; come again evening, take you home."

"But, you young ruffians, what am I to do out here alone? I don't know the way, and I want you to carry my things," expostulated the Englishman, vainly trying to adjust a pair of blue goggles over his eyes, smarting already in the intolerable glare from the sand, while striving not to let drop his camera, fiercely cuddled under one arm, and its tripod of steel legs and an overcoat balanced on the other.

The black remained for a moment impassive, statuesque, wrapped in reflection. Then he brightened:

"Me know," he said, suddenly springing from the boat. "Me take you my house. Sister show you the way: sister carry mister's things."

The Englishman stared for a moment into the eager, intelligent face, strangely handsome, though in ebony. After all, do we not think a well-carved table beautiful, although sometimes, even because, it is in ebony? Then *he* brightened:

"Very good; take me to your house, and let me see your sister," he said good-humouredly; adding inwardly, "If she's anything like you, she'll be the very thing for the camera."

They turned from the cool, rolling, billowy water inwards towards the desert and the huts of Omdurman, and the heat rose up and struck their cheeks each step they took.

*   *   *   *   *

Merla stood that morning at her hut doorway looking out - out towards the river she could not see, for the banks rise and the desert falls slightly behind them. She stood on the threshold, and the sun beat on her Eastern face, and showed it was very good. She was sixteen, and, like her brothers who ran the naphtha launch for the English, she was straight and erect, tall and lithe and supple, with a wonderful stateliness and majesty of carriage, though she had never been taught deportment nor attended physical culture classes. Merla was beautiful, with the perfect beauty of line that belongs to her race, and possessed the straight, high forehead, the broad, calm brow that tells of its intelligence and nobility. She knew, however, nothing of her own beauty. She never cared for staring into the little squares of glass that the girls of the village would buy in the market-place, nor coveted the long strings of blue glass beads that the Bishareens brought in such numbers to sell in Omdurman; nor did it specially please her to lay the beads against her neck, and see them slide up and down on her smooth skin as she breathed, though her companions would thus sit for hours cross-legged before their little mirrors, breathing deep to note how their beads rose and fell and glistened in the light.

Merla loved much better to steal out of the hut at night, when the oil-lamp smoked against the mud wall and the air was heavy, into the pure calm darkness of the desert, and gaze up at the stars, and listen to the far-off tom-toms beating fitfully against the stillness. And if ever any little coins came into her possession, it seemed unkind to spend them on glass or beads when there was always milk and oil needed in the house. And if, when these were bought, there was any coin left, then her real luxury was to buy food for the poor thin camel that lay at night in the mud-yard behind their hut, and to go and feed it secretly in the starlight. And she would press her hands into the soft fur of its neck as it leant towards her, feeling that delight that springs from being kind and loving, and being loved. The law of her life was love, a law springing naturally in her mind, as the beauty and health in her body. Her father, her mother, her brothers were all loved by her; and, beyond these, the unfortunate camels and the donkeys whose sides bled where the girths cut them as the careless Englishmen rode them in and out of the village to and from the Mahdi's tomb, and the lean, barking curs in the mud street that seldom barked as she passed by. All these she loved and sympathised with, though she had not been taught sympathy any more than she had been taught grace.

This morning she was radiant and happy as she looked through the quivering, yellow light that danced above the sand towards the river. Last night she had fed the camel and caressed it, and she had listened, half awe-struck, to the tom-toms in the distance. The music had seemed to come to her ears with a new sound. The breeze had blown from the river with a new kiss to her face. She was growing into a woman, and the sap of life was rising fast and vigorous within her, lifting her up with the boundless joy of life. And as she looked, two white spots, a crested turban and a solar topee, appeared over the edge of the bank, moving towards her.

"My sister!" said the Soudanese boy, with a regal air, when they stood at the mudhouse door. And some instinct, as he was young and foolish, made the Englishman drag off both goggles and solar topee for a moment, and so Merla looked up and saw him with the sun bright on his light Saxon hair and friendly blue eyes.

"Merla," went on the boy rapidly to his sister in his own tongue, "this English mister from Khartoum must have a guide to Kerreree. I go back to the boat: other Englishman want me. You go to Kerreree, Show everything; carry black box for him - carry everything. Salaam, Stanhope Mister."

And, without waiting for either assent or dissent, he swiftly, yet without any loss of dignity or show of hurry, departed. Merla's large eyes were downcast. She was a free woman, and came and went unveiled, nor was it impossible for her to talk to the white people, for her parents were poor and humble, and glad to make piastres in any way they could. One of her sisters was a water-carrier at the hotel in Khartoum, and she might be engaged there also when she was older. But still she held her eyes down, for she felt embarrassed and oppressed, and, besides, the topee and the goggles had been replaced, and they spoilt the vision she had seen first of the English face.

"Well, Merla, if that's your name, will you come with me?" the Englishman said lightly. He knew the tongue well that her brothers spoke, not in any of its refinement and subtlety, but in the ordinary distorted way an Englishman usually speaks a foreign tongue.

"I will ask if I may," she returned simply, in a low voice, and drew back into the dark hut behind her. After a moment she reappeared. "My mother and my brother have ordered it," she said calmly. "I am ready."

Struck by the philosophic, impassive accent of her voice, and not feeling at all flattered, the young man added in rather a nettled tone:

"But I hope it's not disagreeable to you. You are willing to come?"

Then Merla looked at him steadily from under her calm, widely-arching brows: "I am willing." A calm pride enwrapped all her countenance, and it seemed as if she said it somewhat as a victim might say, "I am willing," on being led to the altar of sacrifice. Yet her eyes were radiant, and seemed to smile on him.

The young Englishman was puzzled, as young England mostly is by the East, and, seeing this, the girl added, "Certainly I am willing; it is fated I should go with you. Give me the black box."

But it goes against the grain of an Englishman to let a woman carry his baggage, though he hires her to do it, and he held his camera back from her.

"Take these," he said; "they are lighter," and he gave the little tripod to her, and so they started down the mud sun-baked street that leads through Omdurman to the desert, and out towards the battle-ground of Kerreree. There were few people stirring; the men had already started to their work in the fields by the Nile, or on the river itself, and the women kept within the close darkness of the huts mixing and baking meal for the evening's food. Merla walked on swiftly and silently like a shadow at Stanhope's side through the mud village, and then on into the silent heat of the desert beyond. Here the fury of the sun was intense. The river was out of sight, lying low between its banks. To infinite distance on every side of them stretched the plain, and the soil here was not golden sand, but curiously black, like powdered coal or lava. Not a living thing moved near them; only, far away towards the horizon, now and then passed a string of camels of some Bedouins travelling. They walked on in silence. Stanhope found the walking heavy, as his heeled boots sank into the loose, black soil, and it was difficult to keep up with the swift, easy steps of the bare black feet beside him. His duck suit was damp, and the line of flesh exposed between cuff and glove on his wrist was burnt to a livid red already in the smiting heat. Suddenly Merla's eyes fell on this, and she stopped. Over her head she wore a loose veil of coarse white muslin. As she stopped, she unwound this from her hair, and tore two strips from it. Stanhope stopped too, well pleased at the pause.

"You burn your English skin; the flesh will come off," she said gravely, and before he quite realised it, she had passed one of the muslin strips round and tied it on his wrist. Stanhope's instinct was to protest at once, but there was something in the girl's earnestness and the tender interest with which she put the muslin on his hand that checked him. Also the pain, whenever his sharp cuff touched the seared skin, was unpleasant, and made him really appreciate the improvised protection.

"Your pretty veil, Merla, you've torn it up for me," he remarked regretfully as they started again. Merla glanced at him suddenly; she said nothing, but the pride and joy in her eyes startled the man beside her. He could find no more words, and silence fell on them again till Merla roused him from a reverie by saying indifferently:

"Look! that white heap there - bones, dead men, dead horses. This side, white bones too; many dead here - many bones."

Stanhope looked round. Everywhere, scattered in heaps, shone the white bones. They had come to the edge of the battlefield. Before them rose the little hill of Teb-el-Surgham, crowned by its cairn of black stones and rocks, surrounded by whitened bones and skulls, from the summit of which the English watched the defeat of the Khalifa's force. Stanhope cast his eyes over the dreary, black, blood-soaked plain, on which there was no blade of grass, no plant, no flower - only black rock and white bones, that shimmered together in the torrid heat.

"Horrible! Merla, war is horrible! Come and sit down; I'm dead tired. Let's sit down here against this rock and rest."

Stanhope threw himself down by one of the rocks at the base of the hill, and leant back against it. The girl took her place on the sand opposite him, with her feet tucked under her. Not far from them lay a skull, turned upwards to the glaring sky.

"Will you let me photograph you?" he asked after a minute's gazing at the rich dark beauty of the youthful face, "or is it against your customs?"

"It is against our customs," Merla answered, her hands closing hard on the tripod beside her. What terror it would mean for her to stand before that great black box, and have that evil black eye glare upon her for long seconds! She had seen her countrywomen flee shrieking to their huts, when the Englishmen approached with their black boxes.

"But you will do it for me, won't you?" answered Stanhope persuasively, having set his heart on the picture.

"Yes, I will do it for you; it is right, if you wish it," she answered steadily.

Stanhope accepted at once such a convenient theory, and sprang up to fix the tripod and the camera in order, and the girl sat still on the sand watching him, cold with terror in the burning air.

"Now, pick up that skull and hold it out in your hand, so. Yes, that's right. Now, stand a little further back. Yes, that's perfect."

There was no difficulty in getting her to pose. The natural attitudes of her race are all perfect poses. And Merla stood erect, facing the camera, with the emblem of death in her hand.

"Thank you; I am very much obliged! That'll be a first-rate picture," he said gratefully when he had finished, and Merla sat down with a strange swimming feeling of joy rushing over her. Stanhope was some time fussing with his camera, and putting it back in its case out of the light. Then he wanted lunch, and drew forth a sandwich-case and a wine-flask. The girl would only eat very little, and would not taste the wine. Stanhope, who was very hungry and thirsty, ate all his sandwiches and drank all the wine, and began to feel very bright, refreshed, and exhilarated.

"Do you know you are very beautiful?" he remarked, as he stretched himself comfortably in the shade of the rock and gazed at her, seated sedately on the sand in front of him.

Victoria Cross

"Beautiful?" she repeated slowly, reflectively, "am I? The white camel that lives down by the market square is beautiful, and so was the Mahdi's tomb."

"Well, you are more beautiful even than the white camel or the Mahdi's tomb," returned Stanhope, laughing. "And what do you think of me?" he added curiously. "Where do I come in the list? Somewhere close after the white camel, I hope."

Then, as she gazed at him steadfastly, without replying at all, he felt rather piqued, and took off his blue glasses and squared his fine shoulders against the rock.

"Oh, you!" said the girl softly at last, "You are like nothing on earth, lord! You are like the sun when he first comes over the plain, or the moon at night, when it floats, white and shining, through the blue spaces!"

She sat sedately still, but her breast heaved under the straight, white tunic: her eyes were full of soft fire: her voice was low, and quivered with enthusiasm. Stanhope flushed scarlet. Confused and startled, he stared into her eyes, and so they sat, silent, gazing at each other.

*   *   *   *   *

That same afternoon there was a big fair or bazaar in the trampled mud square in the centre of the Soudanese village that lies higher up the river at the back of Khartoum. The place was gay with colour and crowded with moving figures. From long distances, from far-off villages down and up the river, the natives had come in, either to sell or to buy along the wide, dusty road that went out from either side of the square, leading each way north and south. The mud-huts stood all round the square, backed by some date-palms, for Khartoum and the village behind it are more favoured with shade than sun-baked Omdurman. And in the centre of the square stood or sat the natives, buying and selling, chaffering and gesticulating. Some were Bishareens, with straight forms and features, and black bodies almost covered with long strings and chains of beads. They stood about gracefully to be admired, with their wooly hair fluffed out at right angles to their head, for the occasion. Some were corn-merchants, sitting leisurely before a heap of golden grain piled up loosely on the ground. Others stood by patiently with their fowls or goats or camels, feeding them with green fodder; and others had vivid scarlet rugs and carpets of native make spread out on the uneven ground. And all day long the noise of the merchants, and the cry of the fowls, and the groan of the camels, and the dust of the square, and the smoke of the cooking fires went up from the bazaar.

In one corner of it, on a square of blue carpet, spread beneath his camel's nose, sat a merchant who had been observed to come early to the fair. He appeared to be a man of some substance, for he was clothed, and the camel kneeling beside him was fat and sleek, and would easily make two of the thin camels of Khartoum. Opposite him, sitting on his heels and holding out two lean hands to tend the small fire that smoked between them, was another, obviously poorer, from his smaller amount of dress and flesh.

"It is true: your Merla is the pearl of the desert. I have heard it from my mother," observed the merchant reflectively. "Still, think, my brother, a good riding camel that can be hired out to the Englishmen every day for thirty piastres the day; in a short time you will feed on goat's flesh, and wear boots, with all that money."

The black eyes of the listener sparkled, but he objected shrewdly enough.

"My daughter eats not as much as a camel, and the English want not a camel every day."

The stranger, fat and comfortable-looking, with a certain amount of opulent Oriental good looks, waved his hand with a lordly gesture.

"Let it not be said that Balloon is an oppressor of the poor. Give me the pearl, and this knife shall go with the camel, also this piece of blue carpet - a noble offer, my brother; where will you find such another?"

He drew from his crimson sash a longish knife, keen-bladed, with trueblue, Eastern steel, and having a good bone-handle, on which the fingers clasped easily. The other took the knife and gazed at it intently.

"'Tis but a poor thing," he said at last, indifferently thrusting it into the cloths twisted round his waist. "Yet the camel and the carpet may suit me, and, as you say, you need not the girl at present, I will agree, as I am a poor man, and the poor are ever under the heel of the rich. The girl shall be sent to your house on your return."

"I go now northwards, and shall return by the full moon; disappoint me not, Krino or it shall be evil for you."

"I disappoint no man," replied Krino calmly, taking over from the other the string of the camel, and the fine beast turned its dark, soft head, and looked with liquid eyes on its new owner.

The sky began to show an orange and crimson glow behind the palms, and many cooking-fires now gleamed like spots of blood upon the sand, and the figures still came and went, and talked and bartered, for the goods were not nearly all sold, and the heaps of fine corn were still high in many places, and the fair would go on to-morrow and the next day. But Krino got up and took his way homeward, exulting over his bargain, and leading the camel.

At the same hour, lower down the Nile, at Omdurman, the river lay calm now, without a ripple, and bathed in gold; a stream of liquid gold it seemed, asleep between its deep-green banks, and only now and then did a white-sailed felucca glide by in the golden evening light.

Two figures came down from the desert to the Nile out of the flat, heated air of the plain to the divine freshness by the water. Here, in the cool, golden light, they paused slow and reluctant to part.

"Good-night, Merla! Are you unhappy that I must go?"

The girl raised her face, and looked at him with steadfast eyes.

"The sun gilds the black rock, but the rock cannot expect the sun to stay. I am quite happy. Good-night!"

Another moment and the little launch had sprung out from the deep shadowed bank on to the golden surface, and was steaming, amidst the gold and rosy ripples, back to Khartoum.

When Merla reached the little enclosure of stamped clay round her hut, she saw a new camel feeding there, and cried out for joy. She ran to it and clasped her hands about its velvet neck, and called to her father, as he sat smoking at the doorway, a dozen questions. Where had it come from? Whose was it? But the old man only chuckled and laughed, and would not answer.

"No, no," he thought, watching her with pride, as she played round the camel, "let the maiden wait to know the joy in store for her till the full moon; she is but a child."

Stanhope went that night to a dance at the palace at Khartoum, but he was late in arriving, and seemed very dull and absent-minded when he came, and flattered the women less than usual. "He used to be such a nice boy when he first came here," they complained amongst themselves, "but he was quite horrid to-night - he must be in love," and they all laughed, for every one knew there was no one in Khartoum to fall in love with except themselves, and he had not led any one of them to suppose she was the favoured one.

CHAPTER II

The night was calm, and in the purple, star-filled sky the moon was rising. It was at the full. The naphtha launch was on the river, but it moved silently; current was with it, and the light airs favourable, so there was no need of the engine; one single sail carried the boat easily over the buoyant water. The stars and the rising moon gleamed in the smooth, black ripples. Stanhope sat in the boat thinking, wrapped in a cruel reverie.

He felt he had sailed the craft of his life too near the perilous shore of unconventionality, and now he saw the rocks ahead of him plainly, on which it would be torn in pieces. Yet how to turn back, or move the helm to steer away from them?

"A month ago," he thought, as his eye caught the reflection of the rising moon in the water, "when that moon was young, I was free. Not a soul cared for me, whether I lived or died, and I cared for no one." Now there was one, he knew, who lived upon his coming, whose feet ran to meet him, whose eyes strained their vision to see his first approach. And he, too; he was no longer free. His heart went out to that other heart, beating for him alone so truly, so faithfully, full of such unquestioning adoration and obedience, in mud-walled sun-parched Omdurman.

When the launch touched the bank, he sprang out and walked swiftly up to their usual meeting-place: the deserted mud enclosure of a deserted hut - an unlovely meeting-place enough - but filled with the sweet air of the desert night and the royal light of the stars.

"My lord looks weary to-night," said Merla softly, after they had greeted each other, and had sat down side by side with their backs to the low wall.

"Yes, I am tired with thinking. What is to be the end of this, Merla? Where is our love drifting us to?"

"Why does my lord concern himself with that? We are in the hands of Fate."

Stanhope moved impatiently.

"Our fate is what we make it."

"It is not wise to enquire about our fate," replied Merla, and he saw her face grow grave with resolution in the dim light. "But I can tell you, if you like, what it will be: when you are ready, you will go back to your own people, your own life, and you will be very happy."

"And you - ?" asked Stanhope in a whisper.

"I shall then have lived my life. I shall die and be buried out there," and she motioned to the desert. "I shall have given my lord happiness for a time: think what delight, what honour!"

Stanhope shuddered.

"Don't, don't, I can't bear to hear you; do you ask nothing for yourself from life?"

"Life has given me all now," returned Merla, with a proud smile on her face.

"Why should we not go home to my land together?" said Stanhope passionately, in that sudden revolt against the laws of custom that stirs all humanity at times. "Why should I not take you to live with me for always to be my wife? who would forbid me?"

Merla shook her head, and pressed hard on his hand lying beside her on the sand.

"The sun cannot lift the black rock from the desert and take it to dwell in the blue spaces; neither can the sun stay with the rock. You are grieving for me; do not. I am quite happy. I accept what must be. My life ends when you go."

For a wild moment it seemed to Stanhope that he must dare everything and take her. After all, she was intelligent: she could be educated. She was beautiful, youthful; and what a love she poured out at his feet! - different in calibre, in nature, different, from its root up, from any love he could hope to find again - a love that asked absolutely nothing for itself, not even the right to live, and yet would give its all unquestioningly, unsparingly. It is not a toy to be thrown away lightly, and Stanhope realised this.

"The blue spaces are cold and empty, Merla," he said, suddenly catching her to his breast. "You must come with me."

"No, lord, it is impossible; you speak only for me," whispered Merla, though she clasped his neck tightly. "You must go and live happy, and I shall die happy; even in my grave I shall remember your kisses."

*   *   *   *   *

An hour later, the moon was well up in the sky, though the light was not yet brilliant, and they parted by the wall of the cattle-byre with promises to meet on the morrow, and he turned and left her standing in the shadow; but some instinct moved him, and he returned and kissed her yet again, and said one more farewell; then he took the narrow track leading down to the river, and Merla knew that she must hasten home; for her father, who had been out in the early evening, would be returning. Before she left she turned back once more into the byre, and stood looking at the stars that she had communed with so often: a great sadness fell on her thoughts, a chill as after a final parting. As she turned to go, her eyes fell on a grey patch on the byre floor - his coat! He had left it behind. Merla gave a little laugh as she picked it up: the parting seemed less final now. She would keep it till the morrow. Would he want it? miss it? No, the night was so still and sultry; and, throwing it over her arm, she passed onwards to her hut.

As she neared the enclosure, her heart beat rapidly. A light was burning within the hut, and by the moonlight she saw the great camel moving restlessly in the narrow space outside. Angry voices reached her in sharp discussion - her father's and another. Just inside the enclosure she paused and listened, trembling, uncertain what this unusual clamour and strange voice might mean.

"I gave you my camel, my knife, and my carpet. Where is the Pearl I was promised? Is not the moon at the full?"

Merla heard these words with a thrill passing through every fibre. She knew her father had no pearl in his possession, but was not her name "Pearl of the Desert"? Next there came some confused murmur - seemingly words of apology - in her father's voice that she could not catch, but the stranger interrupted angrily:

"Unhappy man! tricked seller, tricked buyer, would you know where the Pearl is? would you know where your daughter hides? I have heard that she has been seen with a stranger, a white-faced stranger - I know not if he be a leper or an Englishman -" with a bitter laugh, "but in either case I want her not. Come, give me my knife, and I lead off my camel."

Merla's heart failed, for her father gave a shriek as he heard the accusation, and a shower of oaths and imprecations came to her shrinking ears. Nothing was clear any more; there was only clamour and raving in the hut. But once she caught the words, "to the river - does he go to the river?" and above all the storm of words there was the awful sound of the sharpening of a knife.

Like a shadow, noiseless and silent, Merla crept swiftly, under the shade of the camel's body, across the enclosure to the mud partition behind which her youngest brother slept, and roused him. "Nungoon!" she said breathlessly, gripping his shoulder, "take the track to the river, and run for your life. You will overtake the Englishman. Tell him this. 'Merla says: Run to the launch and get off the land quickly, and never come back to Omdurman, or come with a guard. They seek to kill you here.' Go, brother; run!"

The boy, startled from his sleep, gathered himself together and rose. His sister, leaning over him with ashy face and fixed eyes, seemed like Fate itself directing him. Moreover, Oriental youth is accustomed to obey unquestioningly. Without a word, simply with a sign of assent, he fled out of the enclosure, down the track to the river.

Merla stepped back and out of the yard, and stood waiting, silent as before; she had formed her resolution, and all fear was past. The mats in front of the door were suddenly pushed aside, and a streak of light fell across the yard, but it could not touch her, sheltered by the wall. She saw her father rush out, wild-eyed, and the long blade of the knife gleamed blue in the moonlight.

Then, as he dashed through the enclosure entrance, she moved her feet suddenly, scraping the sand, and then fled, wrapped in Stanhope's long light overcoat, up towards the desert, away from the river. Krino, blinded, maddened by passion, glanced at the wall whence came the scraping sound, and then, catching sight of a flying form in English dress, plunged with a cry of triumph after it. Merla fled like the wind along in the shadow of the wall, keeping in the darkness, with her head down, fearing lest her bare head or bare feet might betray her. But Krino's eyes were fixed on the silvery grey of the English overcoat, and, blind to all else, he raced on in the uncertain light with his eyes intent on the shoulders between which he would plunge his knife. Up through the heart of sleeping Omdurman, past silent huts and yellow walls that gleamed pale in the moonlight, through the village to the desert, hunted and hunter fled on, and Krino's heart rose in savage triumph.

"Fool! he cannot escape me now; by the river - yes, but not in the desert; he cannot escape."

And the desert was reached and entered, and still the two noiseless shadows fled over the sand.

Merla's strength was failing: her sight was reeling; she could run no more. Only the joy of knowing that each step led the enemy farther from her loved one had supported her till now. Now he was safe, he must be away on the friendly river. There had been ample time. Not now would it be possible for Krino to reach the river before her lover had embarked. It was well. All was well! And the black sand spun round her in the moonlight, as she heard the hiss of her father's breath behind her. She wavered. With a bound the man threw himself forward. One stab, and the keen blade sank through the flesh below the shoulder, driving her forward, and she fell face downwards on the sand.

Blind still with fury, the Soudanese bent down, tore at the head to drag it back that he might slash it from the body, and turned up the face to the moonlight. Fixed in agony and triumph, it looked back at him - the dead face of his daughter, the PEARL OF THE DESERT.

IV

The last flare of the sunset was falling on the walls of Jerusalem, staining them crimson, and flooding all the enchanting circle of the hills that lie round the city with rosy light. Low down in one of the depressions, where the long sun-rays could not reach, and the olive-trees looked grey in the twilight, stood the grim, white Monastery of the Holy Virgin. The air was sweet and cool here, far from the pollution of the city, and the evening sky stretched fair and radiant above the purple hills. Unbroken quiet reigned, and only one thing in the landscape moved - the figure of a girl ascending swiftly a narrow, stony road under the shadow of the wall. She seemed burdened with many things that she was carrying, and oppressed with some haunting fear, for she looked back frequently, and then pressed on with redoubled speed. The stony track brought her at last to the corner of the enclosure of olive-trees belonging to the monastery; it branched here, one path leading straight to the gates of the building, the other skirting the olive-wood plantation, and then passing on out into the barren hills and open country towards Jericho. The girl took the second track, and here, under the friendly shade of the sheltering trees, she walked more erect and easily. When she reached the farther corner of the plantation she stopped and listened, gazing round her. There was no sound, the light was failing, the hush deepening. "Nicholas," she breathed in a clear whisper, leaning on the low stone plantation wall, "are you there?" A rustling of some long robe against bushes answered her - the olive branches were pushed aside, and the figure of a Greek priest came from between them. With a smile of intense joy on his face he leant over the wall, and clasped the girl's two soft hands in his.

"Esther!" he whispered back, "you have come; you have decided then, you are ready?"

"I am quite ready," answered the girl, pressing close to the wall and lifting her face; the last gleam of gold light from the rising ridge to the west touched it, and showed it was very fair. "If you are sure it is right, if you have faith in Jehovah to lead us."

The priest's face, pale and emaciated, with the rapt look of the visionary stamped upon it, lighted up suddenly with a new exaltation.

"I am quite sure. Last night when I was praying, still in doubt, before the great crucifix, I heard a voice from above saying: 'Nicholas, you are absolved from further prayer and penance here. Go forth with the maiden you love and serve Me in the world. The joy of human hearts singing to Me in grateful praise is more pleasing to Me than these groans and tears and prayers. I have created the blue sky and the laughing seas and the green hills; go forth and see my works, and praise Me.'"

The Jewish girl had listened intently, her face as rapt as his while he spoke, the fire of joy glowing in her eyes.

"Come, then, at once," she murmured in an ardent whisper, and Nicholas stepped over the low boundary into the hill road, now wrapped in darkness. Before them still glimmered dimly the white outlines of the monastery behind the trees. The man stood motionless, gazing at them, the girl's hand tightly clasped in his and held against his breast.

"The agony, the misery I have suffered behind those walls," he muttered, "for sixteen years!"

"It is over," murmured the girl; "come away to the hills; we have no time to lose."

She stooped to gather up the objects in the road. "I have brought you these things," she said confusedly, hardly audibly. "Change into them quickly, and then follow me up the road. No, I will take all the rest," she added, as he took the bundle of clothing she gave him and stretched out his hand for the other smaller things. "Hasten, Nicholas, it is so dangerous here!" With this parting entreaty she went on up the road carrying the bundles.

After she had gone a little way she paused and listened - all was quite still - the stars now showed fitfully in the deepening purple of the sky, a little breeze blew gently up from the wilderness towards Jerusalem. The girl sat down by the wall, with her back against it, and her hands clasped round her knees. Her face had a strange, wonderful beauty as she sat waiting, white-skinned and softly-moulded, with resolute, dark eyebrows drawn straight across the calm forehead. A few moments passed, and then Nicholas approached; his flowing priest's robes were gone, the high, straight, black hat of the order was no longer on his head: it was bare, and the long uncut hair, as the Greeks wear it, was twisted in two thick fair coils round his head. Esther sprang up, untwisting a broad sash from her waist.

"Take this! No wait! let me twist it round your head - yes, so. Now it looks like a Jewish turban. You have the robe and the hat with you? - yes, bring them, bring them," and they hurried on, fleeing away from the monastery. Esther knew a short track across the hills which in a little while joins the great main road to Jericho, that descends down and down through the bare rolling hills of the wilderness to the fair plain of the Jordan and the shores of the Dead Sea. For the first few miles they sped on in silence with clasped hands, the night wind rushing against their faces, and no sound coming to their ears but the occasional whine of the hungry hyenas, prowling over the stony, starlit hills. In the man's breast swelled an exaltation beyond all words: it lifted him up so, that his feet seemed flying over the rugged ground without touching it; the night-wind filled his veins with fire: his brain seemed alight and glowing. For years past the bare stone walls of his monk's cell had given him pictures painted by his fevered fancy of such a walk as this through starlit, open spaces - a walk to life and freedom. For years his hot, caged feet had paced the stone cell floor, aching to pass the threshold; and for the last month ever since from amongst the olive-trees he had seen the fair Jewish girl pass by, a new vision had come upon those white-washed walls to add its torture to the rest. Evening after evening he had stolen out at sunset to see her pass, as she came and went from the little cluster of Jewish houses on the ridge beyond the monastery and watched the sunlight play upon her brows and hair. Could this thing, so divinely beautiful, be the creation of the devil to destroy men's souls? His reason revolted against it. If so, the warm sunlight and radiant sky and air, the flowers and the purple hills, his weary eyes strained out to must be also the devil's work, for all these things were akin, and the woman passing amongst them was but the masterpiece made by the same hand.

"Say," he had said wearily, one night, to a monk passing him like a silent shadow on his way to his cell. "Is all the world the work of the devil?"

"Nay, brother, what blasphemy!" returned the other, startled beyond measure. "It is all the work of God" and Nicholas had passed into his cell well pleased. And the next evening he had called softly to the masterpiece of the Creator, as she went by, and the girl, startled and fearful at first, had spoken a few words out of sheer pity for the hungry, lonely soul looking out so wistfully at her; and then how soon had come other meetings, the plan to escape - that final vision which had seemed to justify him, - and now the flight!

"Will the boat be there! will they wait for us?" he asked eagerly, as they walked swiftly on.

"Yes, I heard the boat was coming over from the Jewish Colony beyond the Dead Sea, and I sent word down it was to take me in it when it left again," the girl replied, "We shall get down there to-morrow evening; we will go to old Solomon's house; he will let us stay with him one night, and in the morning we must get down to the shore and the boat."

Nicholas pressed her hand as they walked on. How wise she was, this little Jewish girl! She had lived her short life in the world, and knew her way about in it so well. And he, so much older, felt like a child beside her, after all those long, deadening, numbing years in the monastery.

Five miles more of the white, stony road were traversed, winding in and out, but always descending between the barren desolate hills of the wilderness, and then Esther said with a little sob in her voice:

"We must stop here now and rest, I am so tired. I cannot go any further to-night."

"Tired?" he echoed wonderingly. Could he ever feel tired now? His feet seemed borne on wings. But he stopped, and bending over her, lifted and carried her tenderly from the starlit road to a large rock jutting out from the hillside. Here, in the shadow on the farther side, they lay down, and the girl fell at once into the deep sleep of utter bodily fatigue. The man lay open-eyed clasping her to him, his brain on fire with freedom, listening with joy to the cries of the wandering wild animals amongst the hills.

The following evening, late, they reached the plain. The wilderness lay behind them, and in front, beyond the green darkness of the trees, they knew the starlight was gleaming on the Dead Sea. The heat down here was suffocating, and their weary feet moved on slowly through the village - a collection of a few white flat-roofed houses, which are all that now mark the spot where stood once the rich, mighty city of Jericho. In the last house shone a light, and Esther led Nicholas towards it.

Solomon was waiting for them, and had prepared for them his best upper room - a little narrow apartment, with windows facing towards the sea - where supper was laid, and opening from this a tiny sleeping chamber. A swinging lamp hung over the centre table, and Solomon's younger brother waited on them. Esther, with the dust of the road washed from her skin, looked very fair, sitting under the light of the lamp, her eyes glowing with the mysterious fires of love and joy, and the two Jews sat listening to her eagerly as she talked to them, telling them the news of her family and friends in Jerusalem.

"If I could only go up to the city," sighed the younger man. "But I cannot walk, and I have no horse," and he grew sullen and dejected and said no more, while the elder continued to ask and be answered a hundred questions about the life and doings of the city.

That night, past midnight, when the whole plain of Jericho lay wrapped in a deep hush, and not one light gleamed in the darkness of the village, a carriage drawn by two foam-covered horses thundered down the last steep descent of the road from Jerusalem into the village, and dashed through it straight to Solomon's dwelling. Esther, asleep in the upper room, with Nicholas' head pillowed on her shoulder, heard the clatter of wheels and awoke suddenly, all her body growing rigid with terror.

"Nicholas, awake! they have followed us!" She sprang from the bed, and opening the window noiselessly, looked out. The night was quite dark, but by straining her eyes she could descry the form of a covered carriage below, and two dark figures stood hammering on the house-door. The sounds rang reverberating through the dwelling, and disturbing the still, calm air without, laden with the scent of myrtle and orange-flower. A window above opened, and the old Jew looked out.

"Who knocks?" he called.

"Priests from Jerusalem, from the Monastery of the Holy Virgin. One whom we seek is within; let us enter." Esther drew back into the room, and saw Nicholas standing behind her, his face haggard with despair. "Jehovah, then, is not with us."

Esther pressed his hand.

"Esther is with you," she murmured softly. "You shall not go back, they shall not touch you. Give me your priest's clothing, and stay here."

Before he could answer she had snatched up the garments and was gone, fastening the door behind her. Outside on the stairway she met old Solomon, coming slowly down to answer the imperative summons from below.

"Delay all you can in admitting them," she whispered, then ran past him, fleet of foot, up the stairs to the Jews' room - the door stood open as Solomon had left it. She entered, and stood within in the darkness.

"Hiram," she called softly, "you wished to go up to Jerusalem. Now is your opportunity. Get up, put on these things, and the priests will take you back in their carriage." She heard the man rise and bound to the floor.

"Is that you, Esther? Have they sent from the monastery to take Nicholas?"

"Yes," returned Esther in an agonised voice. "But you will not let them take him? See, Hiram, they cannot hurt you; they will not recognise you, nor suspect you here in the darkness, in the dress of Nicholas. You need not speak. They will hasten you into the carriage. To-morrow when they discover you, it will be too late for them to overtake us. We shall be gone, and *you* they will not want. They cannot put you in their monastery. They must release you, and you - will be at the gates of Jerusalem."

Her low voice, thrilled with her agony of fear and suspense: there was the very soul of persuasion in it. As she pleaded in the darkness, she heard the man breathing quickly, and shuffling his feet on the floor. He was hesitating. He longed to go up to the city, but this seemed a dangerous expedient. Yet it would serve Esther, and she was very fair, and was of his own kindred. There was a noise and clamour downstairs beneath them - the sound of the slow unbarring of bolts, and angry voices without. Esther drew nearer, and her voice grew sharp with fear:

"Hiram, as they are pushing you to the carriage, I will throw myself into your arms, and you shall kiss me your last farewell, as if you were Nicholas."

In the darkness she felt that the man stretched out his hand.

"Give me the clothes; I will go."

Esther threw them into his arms, and darted out, closing the door, and hung over the stair-rail. There was no light, but she could hear the heavy footsteps coming up. Nearer they came, and nearer, stumbling, and Solomon's step behind, as he followed the priests, grumbling and protesting. Now they were almost opposite the door of the room where Nicholas crouched waiting.

"He is not here! he is not here!" wailed out Esther's voice suddenly from above, and the priests hearing her, rushed up the stairs to where she stood, passing by, forgotten, the door of the lower room.

Rigid and tense she stood before the door as if guarding it, her arms outstretched before it. The first priest pushed her roughly on one side, the second opened the door, and beyond, dimly outlined against the open window square, was visible the draped figure and heavy hat of a priest. With a shout of triumph they darted forward, and Esther gave a great cry of wild despair. The priests dragged him out unresisting, and forced him down the stairs. No word came from him. Solomon, leaning back against the wall to let them pass, stretched out his hand to the weeping Esther; but she passed him, crying and hurrying after her lover. Down in the passage the large door stood wide, showing the waiting carriage in the dim starlight of the sultry night. As they pushed him to the door, he suddenly wrested himself free for an instant, and Esther rushed into his arms.

"Oh, Nicholas, Nicholas! Good-bye!"

The priests seized her by the shoulder, wrenching her away, and one hurled her with a fury of loathing back into the darkness of the passage. Then they forced their prisoner forward, stumbling, resisting, to the carriage. The door snapped to, the horses plunged forward, and the carriage thundered away into the night. Esther picked herself up from where she had fallen in the passage, and bruised and trembling, but with a joyous smile, rushed up the narrow stairway.

"Solomon!" she said, whispering in the old Jew's ear, "Hiram has gone in the place of Nicholas! Nicholas is safe here. Oh, help us to get to the sea!"

Solomon shook with laughter as he heard - for a Jew loves dearly a clever ruse - and he stroked Esther's soft hair as she stood by him.

"Light us a lamp, and let us get away to the shore, that we can embark and be away on the water at dawn, before they discover it and return," Then she passed by him and entered the room where Nicholas awaited her. Solomon trimmed a lamp and a lantern for them, and put up some bread and meat for their journey, his shoulders shaking with inward chuckles as he did so.

"Hiram a priest!" he repeated to himself; "that is a joke indeed, and Esther, what a quick brain she has - a true daughter of Israel!" and Esther was murmuring within to Nicholas:

"Jehovah has saved us. Now let us hasten down to the sea."

The next morning, when the dawn broke soft and rosy over the fair plain of Jericho, the sea that is called the Dead Sea, yet seems, in its glorious wealth of colour and sparkling brilliance to be rather the emblem of Life, glowed and flashed like a huge sapphire in the sun's rays, and at its calm edge, that meets the shore without a ripple, swayed gently the ship of the pilgrims from the Jewish Colony.

Nicholas and Esther sat side by side watching the pilgrims' oars dip quietly in perfect rhythm as they sang. And the song of praise went up through the golden air, and echoed back to the sunny, silent strand vanishing behind them.

V

Dawn was breaking over the desert. Steadily the triumphant rose spread upward in the pale opalescent sky, and broad waves of light rippled slowly over the wide level plain. The little keen breeze of the morning, the herald of the dawn that runs ever in front of its chariot, stirred the branches of the palm trees by the Nile, and played a moment idly with the flap of a tent door before it passed onward. Here, some two miles away from cool Assouan, lying out in the desert, was the Bishareen encampment, and the last small tent of the long line had its door open, and the flap of the awning loose, with which the morning wind stopped to play.

Within, seated cross-legged on the scarlet rug and sheepskin which formed their bed, were two girls braiding their hair before a tiny square of glass, which each in turn held up for the other.

"How cold the morning is! How I hate to hear the wind shake the door flaps," one said and shivered.

"Doolga, don't; you are holding the glass all crooked; I cannot see myself. Why should you feel cold this morning of all others, when Sheik Ilbrahim dar Awaz is coming to claim you?" returned the other, and she laughed softly, with her slim fingers busy trying to bind up and restrain her dusky cloud of hair.

How lovely she was, this young Bishareen, who had looked on

the yearly fall of the Nile but fifteen times - lovely as the tall slender palm of the oasis, or the gold light on the river at sunset. Tall and straight, with the stately carriage and proud head of her race; smooth and supple, with every limb faultlessly moulded under the clear, lustrous skin.

"Silka, Silka! I cannot marry the Sheik. I am in terror of him. Help me, save me!"

The little glass fell on the blanket between them. In the warm rose glow now filling the tent, Doolga's face was ashen-coloured. Awe-struck and startled Silka gazed wide-eyed upon her. For an instant the two girls sat staring in silence into each other's eyes. So much alike they were that one face seemed the reflection of the other, only there was a bloom, a light, a sweetness on Silka's that was missing in the other.

"Why?" she breathed after that first startled silence, "what is the matter, Doolga? Tell me; tell me everything."

She drew nearer her sister, and put one arm round her. The pink light from without, striking through the tent canvas, touched her face, showing its delicately-cut, exquisite features and the tender love filling the eyes.

"I hate the Sheik!" sobbed Doolga, putting down her head on the other's soft bare shoulder; "I don't want him. I love *him*!"

And Silka felt that everything indeed was told. The incoherent, inexplicable words were clear enough to her. She trembled all over, and the two girls clung together in the little tent, while the noise of a large encampment awakening grew about them outside.

Suddenly Doolga grew calm; she lifted her face, and Silka saw it was grey, with great lines of anguish cut in it, and her heart seemed to contract with pain, for she loved Doolga better than anything she knew in the world, and Doolga's suffering was her suffering.

"I thought, father thought you would be glad to marry the Sheik," she faltered.

"I cannot. I will throw myself into the Nile rather; Silka, help me!"

"How can I?"

"*You* marry the Sheik!" Doolga's eyes were alight with flame. Something of the tiger's glare shone in them. She bent forward and seized the other girl's wrists in a feverish grip. The clasp hurt and burnt like fire. Silka drew back instinctively, paling with surprise.

"I marry the Sheik?" she repeated, "but - "

"Yes, you *must*! Oh, Silka, you have always loved me: save me now. I cannot. It will be death to me. I love - I love -" she hesitated; then added, "so much. You love no one. Why not then the Sheik? Do this for me. I will think of you, bless you always. Save me from death; save me from the Nile!"

The burning words, uttered low, in that strange, strained voice she hardly recognised, fell upon Silka like drops of molten lead. Her sister seemed mad: her eyes started forward from her livid face: her clasp on Silka's wrists gripped like iron. Silka's heart was overwhelmed with pity and distress.

"How can I?" she murmured back, bewildered by the sudden revelation of misery in the other - this other that had grown up with her, played with her, slept with her side by side through the soft, hot nights when they had lain counting the stars through a chink in the tent. Side by side their bodies had nestled together, and side by side their hearts had always been.

"You have but to unveil your face to the Sheik," returned the other quickly, eagerly, almost furiously, "and he will take you instead of me. Think, Silka! the head of the tribe, fifty camels, a thousand goats -" She stopped in her eager outpour of persuasion. Silka was looking at her straight from under her dark, level brows, her lips curled in a sorrowful disdain.

"Have his riches any weight with you, Doolga? Why do you offer them to me?" she said proudly.

"Because you are free: you do not love," impetuously returned the other with glib, persistent vehemence. "I would marry the Sheik, I would prize his flocks, his riches; but I love - I love - I cannot!"

"Whom do you love so much?" replied Silka sadly. "Why have you not told me? Who is he?"

The girls were seated on the bed in one corner of the tent close beside its stretched canvas wall. There was a little eyelet, a square hole with a flap buttoned down over it, on a level with their heads. At Silka's question Doolga turned to the canvas, and, with an impatient movement, tore up the flap and looked out. The plain was bathed in gold: above, the pure, pink glow still hung in the limpid sky. The encampment was astir. The tents were open, and little cooking fires, sending up their spirals of blue smoke were dotted over the sand. At a few paces' distance from the main row of tents, the camels, lying down, made a velvet-like patch of shade on the gleaming gold of the sand, and herds of white goats stood near, their silky coats flashing in the morning sunlight. Silka looked out, too, over her sister's shoulder. She saw the burnished gold of the plain and the luminous sky, and between these two a figure that stood by a low brown tent, with the sunlight falling full on its noble brow and the straight profile turned towards them. Doolga wrung Silka's hand, that she still clutched, as they knelt side by side on the sheepskin looking through the eyelet.

"That is he!" she said, and Silka's lips parted suddenly in a little scream of pain.

"What is the matter?" asked Doolga roughly, drawing her back from the aperture, and letting the flap fall.

"You hurt me," replied Silka. "Is that the one you love?" Her voice sounded tremulous: her eyes, fixed on Doolga, seemed to widen with increasing pain.

"Yes, that is he; that is Melun," answered Doolga softly. "Is he not handsome, wonderful? Why do you stare so? Might not any girl love him?"

A little smile played round Silka's lips.

"Yes, indeed, any girl might love him," she answered.

"But not as I do - no, never! Oh, Silka, I cannot tell you how I love him. More than the Nile, more than the stars, more than we have ever loved each other! I have met him often when I went to draw water, and sometimes we have stayed together in the palm-grove. I was so happy till father sold me to the Sheik; and now I must part from Melun for ever! Do not make me, dear, darling Silka; do not send me to the Nile!" She spoke with increasing excitement, with passionate intensity. She was close to Silka, and she laid one arm softly round her neck and put her face close to hers. Such a beautiful oval face it was! - the face that Silka loved: as she looked at it, her heart melted within her.

"See, dearest Silka," continued the other coaxingly, "you have nothing to do but to unveil before the Sheik; you are just like me, only a thousand times lovelier. He will not want me then, but you. You can say to our father: As I am fairer than my sister, he will give you two more camels. Father will be pleased with the camels, and I shall be left free to marry Melun."

"But suppose I don't want to marry the Sheik either," said Silka, slowly stroking the curls of the sheepskin as she looked down upon it.

"But why should you not? he has flocks and herds; he will give you necklets and bracelets, and a camel to ride, and take you to the oasis? Why should you mind?"

"It is late, Doolga. Father will be returning soon. Go, fill your urns at the well."

"But will you promise - ?"

"I can promise nothing yet. Go, go, leave me, you must let me think a little."

Doolga got up well satisfied. She knew Silka had never refused her anything since they had first played as babies together in the sand. Silka loved her. Silka had never denied her anything.

She took her large earthenware jar, poised it on her shoulder, and went out of the tent into the hot light. Silka lay on the sheepskin where her sister had left her, and turned her face to it, shaken with a storm of feeling that convulsed her slender body from head to foot. She heard none of the cheerful sounds of life stirring round the tent; she heard only Doolga's threat of the Nile, her passionate pleading for help. Her face was buried in the sheepskin, yet she saw plainly in the wall of darkness before her eyeballs the figure of the Bishareen standing out against the pink light of the morning sky. So it was Melun that Doolga loved! And to Melun all her own passionate impulsive heart had been given through her eyes. Had she not, morning after morning, gazed out through the square eyelet to catch a glimpse of him as he came from his tent, dressed in his snowy white linen tunic, and with countless strings of coloured beads twisted round the firm column of his throat and hanging from his arms? Melun, the necklace-seller of Assouan! Melun, that the foreign tourists stopped to gaze after, as he walked with slow and stately steps beneath the lebek trees on the "boulvard" by the Nile. Young and straight and slender, with a beautiful face and form, he never offered his wares for sale. He simply stood and looked at the tourists, and they came and bought largely. They came up to him with curious eyes to chaffer for his blue-glass beads, and stare at his smooth, perfectly-moulded arms and throat, at the wonderfully straight features, and the lofty carriage of his head, at the thick hair, like fine, black wool, that waved above his forehead and clustered round the nape of his neck, interwoven with his brilliant blue beads. Ah! how she loved Melun! how she had dreamed of the day when her elder sister, happily married, she herself could go to her father and say, "Let Melun, the necklace-seller, come to the tent and see my face." And now, not for him, but for the old hard-visaged Sheik, she was asked to unveil. "I cannot do it; no, I cannot," she muttered to herself, and the thought of Melun came to her softly. "I have but to look at him, and he must love me; he is mine." Did not her mirror tell her this each morning? Had not her sister but now said the same? She smiled to herself, and balm seemed poured through her. Then there came another thought piercing her like a dagger. Melun is not mine, but hers. She loves him; he loves her. They have met in the palm-grove. Never, never, could she unveil for him now. He must never see her. Though he loved her a thousand times, yet would she never take him from Doolga. Doolga, bright, graceful, and beautiful, the light of her eyes, the joy of the tent! could she bear to see her brought through the door cold, motionless, lifeless, killed by the embrace of the Nile?

When Doolga returned with the flush of warmth on her cheek and the jar full of shimmering water on her shoulder, Silka was sitting upright on the bed with dry, wide eyes. One glance at her told Doolga that she herself was free, that the other would take up her burden and bear it for her. She crossed over with a quick beautiful movement, lithe, free, untamed.

"Darling Silka, you will consent? you will promise?"

"Do you meet him often in the palm-grove?" returned Silka; it was now her eyes that were full of flame as she met her sister's.

"Why - Melun? Yes, whenever it was possible. To-night there will be no moon; I was going, but why should you ask?" She bent forward quickly, eagerly, some faint suspicion stirring in her.

"If I do this for you - if I save you - if I show myself to the

Sheik, then you must let me go to the palm-grove to-night."

Doolga fell back from her, surprise and terror and horror mingling in her face. She clasped her small, soft hands together and wrung them.

"Oh, Silka! you know, if he sees you, he will not look at me again; he will not care."

Silka smiled a slow, painful smile.

"Do you not see?" she said in a whisper. "I shall go as you. Who will know it is not you? Not Melun. He will be expecting you! He has never seen me. I will not betray myself nor you, but this is my condition. To-morrow I go in your stead to the Sheik; to-night, I go in your stead to Melun."

Doolga stared at her, barely comprehending.

"But why - why?" she stammered in return.

"I go to the Sheik in your stead because I love you, and to Melun in your stead because I love him," replied Silka firmly.

There was a smile in her eyes, but her lips were pale, compressed, and sad. Doolga gazed at her in silence, both hands clasped tightly now over her swelling breast. Astonishment, gratitude, mistrust, and jealousy were all struggling together within it for mastery.

"You love Melun too?" she said at last. "Then why do you not take him? One glance from you and he is yours."

"He was yours first," answered Silka miserably. "I cannot take him from you."

"And you will marry the Sheik to save me?"

"Yes," replied Silka.

Then Doolga fell on her knees and thanked Silka and kissed her, and Doolga's kisses were very sweet, and while those lips pressed hers Silka forgot everything else in the world. At last Doolga said in a sudden recrudescence of jealousy:

"In the grove to-night you will not -" and the rest was whispered.

"No," answered Silka; "I am the bride of the Sheik. You need fear nothing. But I must see Melun; all my life long I shall feed on your happiness. There will be nothing else for me. I shall live on it. To do this I must have a vision of it before I go, and it will stay by me for ever."

That afternoon the tent was gay with unrolled silks and scarlet rugs, and coffee stood out in little porcelain cups upon the floor, for the Sheik Ilbrahim had come to the final parley for his bride. He sat before the coffee-cups on a black goat-skin, the pipe of honour placed beside him. A grave, quiet man, with kind eyes, but already far on in the winter of life. Opposite him sat his host, the owner of the tent and father of the girls. Shrewd-eyed, keen-faced, quietly he did his bargaining. Earlier in the day the elder girl had laid the plan before him: herself for Melun, the necklace-seller of Assouan, who owned neither camels nor goats, but would pay well in silver straight from the hands of the tourists; her younger sister for the Sheik, who would give doubtless two more camels for her wonderful beauty. The father listened placidly. It was not a bad bargain.

"But," he answered finally, "why should you not go to the Sheik now for two camels and by and by another will come for your sister and give four camels. Then shall I have had six for the two of you."

"But she may die," objected the ready Doolga, the keen-witted daughter of her father. "Better secure the camels now, father."

"True, she may die, and the bargain be lost," mused the father, and at last he spread out his hands with a gesture of conclusion.

"It is for the Sheik to decide," he said merely, and Doolga was content. She knew beforehand what the Sheik would decide when he saw her sister. Now the two girls sat clasped in each other's arms behind a curtain hung across a corner of the tent, and waited silently till they should be summoned.

"If she be fairer than your daughter Doolga," they heard the Sheik say good-humouredly, "she must be fair indeed, and worth four camels. Let me see her."

At those words Silka rose and stepped from behind the little curtain. With timid steps she came forward to the centre of the tent. A linen tunic clasped round the base of her throat fell almost to her ankles, caught lightly in at the waist by a scarlet cord; loose sleeves falling from the shoulder half-concealed her rounded arms; but her lovely face, with its arching brows and liquid eyes, looked out unveiled from her frame of cloudy hair, and drew the Sheik's heart towards her. Wrapt in the enthusiasm of the holiest of all loves, that of sister for sister, tense with the ardour of her sacrifice, a light shone out from the tender soul within that fired all her beauty, making it burn like the sun, and intoxicate like wine.

Her father eyed her, and wished he had asked five camels.

The Sheik stretched out his right hand towards her.

"Are you pleased to come, my daughter, to the oasis of roses with me?"

"My lord beholds his slave," answered Silka, and her eyes were full of light, and her lips were curved in smiles.

"My camels, four of the best, will find their stable behind your tent to-night," said the Sheik to her father, and he filled the cup he had drunk from and handed it to the girl. Silka raised it to her lips.

"Does it please my lord that he fetch me to-morrow, and leave me in my father's tent to-night?"

The Sheik laughed good-naturedly, his eyes fixed on the pleading, youthful face.

"It pleases me not to leave you; but if you ask me, little one, I will not refuse. Let it be so."

As he spoke Silka drained the coffee-cup he had given her, and by so doing bound herself to him henceforward.

There was no moon that night; it was dark with the darkness of the desert, and the splendour of its million stars. As Silka came softly from the tent she looked upwards; the wild heaving of her bosom seemed repeated in that restless, pulsing light above. The soft breath of the desert came to her; it whispered of Melun waiting for her in the palm-grove. How happy she was! This was life: one night of life was hers - no more. With the dawn came the end. This was her first - her last - night of life, but how exquisite it was! The voice of the desert sang in her ears, the light soft sand caressed her flying feet. Within bounded her heart, buoyant with leaping joy. Never had she realised the strength of her swift, straight ankles - never till now the free, joyous power in her supple limbs.

Before her rose the palm-grove, distinct in all its beauty of feathery-topped trees, against the gorgeous starlit sky. By her side gleamed now the line of the river, silver in the starlight; smooth and lovely, studded with its fierce black rocks, flanked by its orange sand, and here and there, on its edge in the radiant darkness, rose a lofty palm lifting its swaying branches towards the jewelled sky. Silka looked at the river curiously. Now she was keenly alive; life was sharp and alert in every fibre, but it was the last. This night of life was also a night of good-byes. To-morrow she would look on the river again, but she would be dead then - dead to joy and to love; it would only be Doolga who would be living rich in both these gifts - gifts given by her. The thought ran through her with a tumultuous gladness.

She entered the palm-grove and went straight to the tree that Doolga had told her of, a withered palm. A figure sat at the foot of the tree. The starlight gleamed on its white clothing. Silka's feet stopped mechanically as she saw him; her heart beat so that she could scarcely breathe; but he had caught sight of her, and sprang to his feet and came towards her. How wonderful he was with his fine head set on that long, firm throat, and how sweet the face when his beautiful mouth broke into smiles as he saw her!

"Doolga!" he exclaimed, and then paused. She heard the little note of wonder, of joy, in his voice, as she looked up at him in the soft starlight, filtered through the palms. She was close to him, and his voice, his presence was a new wonder to her.

"You are lovelier to-night than ever before. You have a new beauty, what is it?" and he stretched out his arms passionately to her and enfolded her in them close to his breast and kissed her. Then in one moment did the rose of life, that unfolds slowly for most mortals petal by petal, bloom suddenly for her whole and complete, and fill her with its wild fragrance, overwhelming her senses. The happiness of a hundred lives was compressed into that one perfect moment when his lips touched hers, and she saw his face hang over hers in the starlight, blazing with the fires of love.

"This then is life," she thought, as she put her arms round his neck. "This is what I am giving to Doolga."

"Am I really more beautiful to-night than I have been?" she asked presently, as they sat crouched close side by side at the foot of the palm, looking towards the silver river.

"A thousand times!" he answered passionately. "I have never loved you, never seen you as I do to-night."

"Then you must always remember me as you see me now. However Doolga looks to you in the future, always remember this night, and how you loved her then."

And he took her more closely into his arms, and pressed kisses on her eyes, and told her in low murmured words of the tent he was preparing for her, pitched where the cool breeze from the Nile would reach them, and of the coming sunsets when she would sit awaiting his return in the doorway, and of the still radiant hours of the desert night which would pass over them full of delirious joys; and the girl listened and lived out her life in those moments against his heart. And ever as she listened, the thought of the Sheik and his withered arms rose before her. Still it was Doolga's future she looked into, the secrets of Doolga's happiness she learned. As often as he murmured, "Doolga!" and caressed her, a wave of joy passed through her.

Three hours before the dawn they parted, and with slow, sad steps she returned to her father's tent. Her strength was spent. Life and she had finally separated. Entering the tent with noiseless feet, no sound disturbed the sleeping chief, and she crept to where her sister sat up, wild-eyed and sleepless, on the bed.

"This he gave to Doolga," she said, with her lips pressed to Doolga's ear, and passed over her head a necklace of faultless beads of jade.

*   *   *   *   *

The following day, when the last flare of the sunset lit up the sky with flame, and the delicate branches of the palms of the oasis showed before them tipped with gold, the Sheik Ilbrahim bent over his bride sitting before him on the camel, decked out with gold ornaments in her hair. He saw her smiling, and a glory that was not of the sunset on her face.

"Of what is my beloved one thinking?" he asked her.

She looked up, but she did not see his face above her. She saw only the tent where the wind from the Nile could come, and Doolga within radiant with the joy she had given her.

"Of what should your slave be thinking, lord," she answered, "but love and happiness?"

VI

It was evening. A sky of purest emerald, luminous, transparent, and divinely calm, stretched over the city of Damascus, that lies in its white glory, wrapped round by its mantle of foliage, in the heart of the burning desert - unhurt, cool, invulnerable in the jaws of the all-devouring desert sand. In the East, with the first cool breath of evening comes a spirit of rejoicing: the heat and burden of the day are over, and there is one hour of pure delight before the darkness. This hour had come to Damascus: the roses lifted their heads in the garden, the birds burst into joyous floods of song, and the trees waved and spread their branches to the little breeze that came rippling through the crystal air.

Almost on the confines of the city, where the belt of protecting verdure grows thin and the gaunt face of the desert presses against the city walls, rose the square, white dwelling of Ahmed Ali, and his garden was the largest and most beautiful of the city. High white walls enclosed it on every side, and from the broad, travelled highway that ran beside it the dusty and wearied wayfarer often lifted his eyes to the profusion of gay roses, the syringa, and star-eyed jasmine that tumbled jubilantly over the edge, and hung their scented wreaths far above his head. The tinkling of a fountain could be heard within, and the mad rapture of song from the birds in the evening, when the scent of the orange blossom stole softly out on the radiant golden air. On the other side of the garden was a grove of orange-trees. The rich, glossy, green foliage rose in dark masses above the high wall, and some inquisitive, encroaching boughs stretched over and occasionally dropped their golden fruit into Ahmed's garden. On the inside of the old, moss-grown wall were numerous buttresses, and in these angles and corners, sheltered from any breeze, the roses and the small fruit-trees fairly rioted together, blending their masses of pink and white bloom.

On this evening, when the sky shone like one sheet of purest mother-of-pearl, green and rose and faint purple, the garden was very still; the only sound was the murmur of the falling water, the coo of some white doves in a pear-tree, and a very light step pacing on the tiny narrow path that wound its way round the whole garden amongst the rose-bushes and lemon-trees.

Dilama, the youngest of the ladies of the harem, was walking in the garden with her white veil thrown back and a smile on her small, red, curling lips. She stooped here and there to gather a flower whenever a bud or blossom of particular beauty caught her eye, and fastened now one against her thick brown hair, and now one or two upon the rich-embroidered muslin that covered the upper part of her bosom. She was intensely happy: in the spring at Damascus, at seventeen and in love, who would not be happy? The fires of youth and love and joy burned in her flesh and danced in her veins and shone in her eyes, and she sang and smiled to herself as she gathered the flowers. She was a Druze woman, and gifted with the wonderful beauty that Nature has showered on the women of Syria. Skins that the most perfect Saxon skin of milk and rose can scarcely rival are wedded to eyes of Eastern midnight and brown tresses filled with shining lights of red and gold. She had been born in the fierce, barren mountains lying behind Beirut, and at eight years old had drifted - part of the spoils of a raid - into the keeping of Ahmed Ali, the richest landowner and merchant of Damascus. He was a Turk, of pure Turkish blood, and with the large, generous heart and the kindly nature of the Turk. All the life that owed him allegiance, that was supported by his hand, was happy and well cared for - from the magnificent black horses, ignorant of whip and spur, that filled his stables, and the dogs that lay peacefully about in his palace, to the beauties of the harem, who tripped about gaily singing and laughing in their cool halls and shaded garden. Where the Turk rules there is usually peace, for his nature is pacific, and in the palace of Ahmed there was joy and peace and love and pleasure in abundance. There were seven ladies of the harem, including Dilama, and six of these were happy wives of Ahmed. Each had one or more sons, handsome, large-eyed, sedate little Mohammedans, who were being trained by Turkish mothers in all sorts of gentle ways and manners - in thought and care for others, in courtesy and kindness; and who were very different in their childish work and play from the brawling, selfish, cruel little monsters that European children of the same age mostly are. But Dilama was not yet Ahmed's wife; she loved him most truly and deeply as an affectionate daughter. For who could not love Ahmed? There was a charm in his stately beauty of face and figure, in the kind musical voice, in the eyes so large and dark and gentle, that was irresistible. But to Dilama he was something far above her: her king, her lord indeed, for whom she would lay down life itself without question, but not the man to whom her ardent simple nature had turned for love. Ahmed had not sought her. When first she came to his palace she had been too young except for him to treat as a pretty child, and the relationship of father and daughter then established had never yet been broken in upon. And the light-hearted, sunny-natured Druze girl had taken life just as she found it, regarding herself as Ahmed's daughter, and rejoicing in her home of love and beauty she ceased to remember that one day he would inevitably claim her as his wife, and that that day must be the beginning or the end of happiness just as she prepared for it. But she did not prepare for it, she ignored it: flitting like some golden butterfly through the pleasant hours, and growing fairer every day, so that the harem women looked at her with a little sinking of the heart yet no ill-will, and said amongst themselves, "Surely Ahmed must choose her soon." But Ahmed loved at that time with his whole soul a Turkish woman, and she was to give him shortly a second child, and for fear of disturbing her peace of mind Ahmed remained in the Selamlik, and would not visit his other wives, nor send for Dilama, though his eyes, like the others, noted her growing beauty day by day.

"I will wait in patience," he thought, looking out one morning at sunrise, and watching Dilama playing with the white doves on the basin edge of the fountain. "I will wait till Buldoula is well and strong again. She would fret now, and think I was forgetting her in a new love if I call Dilama to me yet. I will wait till her second son is born, and then in her joy and pride she will not be jealous of the new wife."

So he waited, but in the game of love he that waits is ever the loser. That night, when the moon was rising over the white and deep green of Damascus, Dilama walked, humming to herself, in the garden, full of a great leaping desire, born of her youth and fine health and the breath of the May night, to love and be loved. Suddenly, when she came to the corner, under the drooping boughs of the grove without the garden, an orange fell, and, just escaping her head struck her heavily on her bosom. With a great shock she stood still, looking up, and there, on the summit of the high wall, amid the green boughs, was a man sitting, leaning over down towards her, with fiery eyes looking upon her from under a dark green turban.

"It is death to be here," she whispered, her face pallid in the moonlight, "do not stay;" yet her whole being leapt up with hope that he would disobey. The man laughed softly.

"It is life to look on you," he said merely, and to her terrified joy and horrified delight he slid down between the lemon-trees and the wall, and stood before her in the angle it made, where two buttresses jutting forward hid him from all view unless one stood directly opposite.

Dilama shook from head to foot; in one fierce, sweeping rush, love passed over and through her as she stood staring with wild dilated eyes on the form before her. Tall, tall as Ahmed, with all the grace and strength of youth, lithe and supple, with a straight-lined, dark-browed face above a stately throat, and dark kindling eyes, wells of living fire that called all her soul and heart and womanhood into life.

"I have often watched you walking in the garden," he murmured, gently taking in his, one nerveless hand. "I come from your village in the hills, where you were taken from long ago. I am a Druze," and he threw his head higher, as the stag of the forest throws his at the first note of the challenge. Dilama knew well that he was of her own people. Infant memories, instinctive, implanted consciousness told her this without the aid of Druze clothing, or the short, gay dagger thrust into his waist-sash.

"I think you are not yet the wife of Ahmed Ali?" he went on, as she simply trembled in silence, wave after wave of emotion passing through her, striking her heart and choking her voice. "Tell me?"

Dilama shook her head, and a triumphant smile curved the handsome lips before her.

"I knew it; you are mine," he said, in reply, and, bending over her as she stood shrinking, on the verge of fainting, between terror and wonder and joy, he kissed her on the lips, not roughly - even gently - but with such a fire of life on his that it seemed to the girl, in the destruction of all her usual feelings, in the havoc of the new ones called in their place, that the actual moment of dissolution had come.

That had been some three weeks ago, and now, on this soft, pearly evening, she was waiting eagerly for the sky to deepen, and the light of the stars to sharpen, and the orange to fall over the wall. For the Druze had come many times, and no one had discovered the lovers, screened by masses of roses in the buttress-sheltered corner of the wall. In fact, for the last weeks no one had had time or thought for anything but Buldoula, who lay sick within the palace walls, and attendants waited anxiously or ran hither and thither on various errands, and Ahmed was in the depths of anxiety; and no one thought about Dilama or paid any attention to her, and she was radiantly happy and self-engrossed, and came and went between the garden and her own little chamber as she listed, undisturbed. And this evening, as usual, she slipped unobserved amongst the roses into the corner of the buttressed wall. A moment after the boughs overhead parted, and the lithe Druze dropped down noiselessly beside her. She put her gold braceleted arms round his strong brown neck, and pressed her silken-covered bosom hard against his rough cotton tunic. A great rush of rosy light flooded all the sky for some minutes, then began to pale softly before the approach of the lustrous purple dark.

In the palace a light behind one of the mushrabeared windows was extinguished; there was the sound of the scurry of feet, and then a long wail came out from the building, rending the pink-hued twilight.

"Buldoula is dead!" remarked Dilama simply, as the lovers crouched together between the wall and the roses. It meant nothing to her, enclosed in the happy warmth of her lover's arms; death had no meaning for her yet, hardly seventeen years' journey distant from birth, and full of all the sap and great leaping fires of life. Death was something so far away, so impossible to realise. It was but a word to her - a casket enclosing nothing. Yet the death of Buldoula was the embryo event in the womb of time from which was to develop the whole tragedy of her own life.

"Buldoula is dead," she said again, carelessly, her rose-tipped fingers smoothing the black sweeping arch of the man's brows. "Perhaps her son is dead also. Ahmed will be very grieved - she was going to bear her second son."

"Little dove! I must take you away to the mountains soon," said the Druze, clasping her tighter to him. "Soon," he muttered again, stooping down to look under the rose-boughs to the white-faced house, now, with all its screened windows, dark. His words seemed irrelevant, yet they were not. He had a keen prescience that the death of the favourite of the harem might influence very quickly Dilama's fate.

"Why not take me now, Murad? I want to see the mountains," and she laid her little head, crowned by its masses of brown-gold hair, on his warm breast.

"The caravan does not start for two weeks more," he answered thoughtfully. "We must wait for it. It would be madness to try to escape alone. We should be seen, noted, and tracked down. Think how Ahmed will look for his treasure when he finds it stolen! But if you are hidden in a bale of goods on a camel in the caravan, who will suspect, who will know that the Druze has taken you? The whole caravan of Druzes cannot be stopped because Ahmed has lost a wife! No, in the caravan, with all the rest, we are safe. There is no other way."

There was silence while the twilight deepened in the garden, and the stars began to show above like flashing swords in the sky. In the languor of love that knows no fear and has no cares, that opiate of the soul, Dilama lay in his arms and sought his lips and eyes, and asked no more about caravans and journeys and mountains, drugged and heavy with love. In an hour when all was velvet blackness beneath the wall, they kissed farewell. He scaled the crumbling bricks, and regained the sheltering orange grove, and she walked slowly back, drawing smooth her filmy veil, towards the darkened palace.

Five days later at noontime, as Dilama was sitting in the garden playing with the tame white doves by the fountain, one of the black female slaves approached her. Dilama looked up questioningly, holding a dove to her bosom.

"The lord is sorrowing within for his dead wife and dead son. He has sent for you; go in, and lead him away from grief," and the woman smiled and prostrated herself before Dilama, who shrank instinctively away like a frightened child. But there is only one law and one will in the harem, and she rose obediently, letting the dove go, and stood ready to follow the slave. That meaning smile on the woman's face filled her with an intuitive, instinctive, undefined fear, and at the same instant there rushed over her the realisation of the great happiness that same smile would have brought her had there been no Murad, had she fled from that rose-filled corner on that first evening - had she, in a word, *waited*! This summons to the presence of their lord is what so many of the harem slaves pine and long for through weary months, and sometimes years. It came now to her, and it meant nothing but vague fear and dread. She followed the slave with unelastic steps, and her brain full of heavy thoughts; they passed the women's apartments and went on to the Selamlik and to the room of Ahmed, that looked out with unscreened windows into the cool, deep green of the garden. The slave drew back at the door, holding a curtain aside for the girl to enter. She went forward, the curtain fell behind her, and she was alone with Ahmed.

He was sitting opposite on a low divan or couch, clothed from head to foot in a deep blue robe, and with a turban of the same colour twisted above his level brows - a kingly, majestic figure, and the girl's heart beat and her eyelids fell as she crept slowly over the floor towards him. At his feet she sank to her knees, and would have put her forehead to the ground, but Ahmed bent forward, and clasping both her arms lifted her on to the couch beside him.

"And you are the Druze child, Dilama?" he said gently, and leaning a little back from her, surveyed her intently with dark lustrous eyes. The girl felt swooning with terror; before his gaze her very flesh seemed dissolving. It seemed as if her heart, her brain, with the image of Murad stamped on them, would be laid bare to those brilliant, searching eyes. What would he not know, suspect, find out? What would he ask? demand of her? She could not ask herself. Was this to be the end of his paternal relationship to her? The beginning of a new one? She dared not lift her eyes lest he should see their terror; the blood burnt in the surface of all her fair skin, as if red-hot irons were pressed to it. And Ahmed, gazing upon her with the pure noonday light, softened by the leafy screen without pouring over her, drank in her fair Syrian beauty with delight. The pale, rose-hued silken clothing she wore harmonised with the ivory and rose of her round arms and throat and cheeks, and threw up the masses of dark hair that fell beneath her veil to her slender waist. Ahmed very gently unbound the snowy garment from her head and stroked her hair lightly, watching the gold gleams in its ripples as his hand passed over them. He saw her dismay, confusion, even her terror, and noticed the quiver of her hands and the irregular leap of her bosom, but these did not dismay him. He was accustomed to be beloved even as he loved, and the women of the harem who came to him in fear left him with happy confidence. He affected now not to see her embarrassment, thinking it to be only that, and said quietly, "And you have been happy, Dilama, in my house?" The girl felt she must speak, though her throat seemed closed and her tongue nerveless.

"Very happy," she faltered at last in a whisper.

"But you have been lonely, perhaps?" he asked. "Have the roses and doves in the garden been companions enough for you? Have you not been too much alone?"

In the heavy load of apprehension of intangible fear and horror that seemed stifling her, a madness of longing came over the girl to be free from her guilty secret, to have never known Murad. Now she could have looked up fearless, full of expectant joy! She could have loved this man; she knew it, now that she felt his love approaching her: hope was dying within her that ever again would he regard her simply as his daughter. She knew those tones of the voice, she had heard them from Murad in the garden, but here the voice was infinitely more refined, the sound of it exquisitely musical; and now, that love for her was in it, it told her a new secret, that she could have given love for love. She knew, though her eyelids were down, how beautiful the face was that bent over her: the straight, severe lines of it, the magnificent eyes and brows burnt through her lids. Ah, why had he waited so long, or she not waited longer?

Full of intolerable, irrepressible pain, she looked up at last suddenly.

"Why did not my lord come into the garden, to the roses and doves and - me?" she asked falteringly, her gaze held now irresistibly by the dark orbs above her. Then, afraid of her own temerity, she became white as death under his gaze.

But Ahmed was rather pleased by this first connected speech she had made in the interview. It sounded to him like the tender reproach of an amorous, expectant maiden, waiting eagerly for her love, too long delayed. The under-meaning, the terrible regret for irrevocable ill, naturally escaped him. He smiled, and put his arm round her shoulders. "Well, it is not too late," he said, bending over her. But the girl shrank from his arm, and he realised it instantly. He was aware directly that there was some feeling in her not quite fathomed nor understood. It puzzled him. He was far too deep a thinker, far too refined a nature to treat his women as inanimate toys to be used for his amusement, either with or without their consent, as the chance might be. He knew them to be, and treated them as, individual souls, with right of will and desire equal to his own, and was too proud to accept the gift of the body unless he had first conquered the will. But usually there was no difficulty. Nature had gifted Ahmed with all the best treasures in her jewel-box; beauty of face and form, strength and grace, charm of voice and presence - everything needed to ensnare and delight the senses, and he was accustomed to be loved, passionately adored, and worshipped. He was naturally a connoisseur in such matters, and knew well and easily the truth or dissembling in them. But here there was neither: the girl shrank from him instinctively, and seemed possessed by nothing but dumb, helpless fear that was distressing to him. Yet not all distressing, for even in the best of male natures there always remains some of the instinctive desire of conquest, the delight in opposition, if not too prolonged, the love of battle, the hope of victory; and to Ahmed, the invariably successful lover, the resistance of this slight, rose-leaf creature he could crush with one blow of his hand roused suddenly all the primitive joy of the chase, the excitement of pursuit. Only, where with some natures it would have been brutal and rapid, the end and triumph assured, the prize the body; here it would be gentle and dexterous, the end dependent on another, the prize the soul - the soul, the will, the most difficult quarry to capture, as Ahmed knew.

He let his arm slip from her shoulders, and rose and walked over to the window, looking out for a moment into the delicious green beyond. Dilama half-sat, half-crouched upon the divan, not daring to stir, and watched him furtively.

Ahmed stood for a moment, and there was dead silence in the room. Then he returned and came towards the couch, standing opposite it, and looking down at her.

"Dilama, you seem very much afraid of me, and why is it? Look up and speak to me. There is no need for fear. Do you think I have called you here to force you to love me? There is no way of forcing love. You are free to come and go to and from this room as you will, but I am lonely and grieved, now Buldoula has been taken away from me. I would like you to come here and play and sing to me, and console me; will you?"

Dilama ventured to lift her eyes to the kingly figure before her, and meeting the pained, dark eyes bent on her, and realising that there was nothing, indeed, to make her fear but her own guilty conscience, she burst suddenly into an uncontrollable passion of weeping, and slipping from the couch fell sobbing at his feet.

Ahmed stooped and gathered her up in his arms, holding her to his breast, and this time she did not shrink from him, but lay there unresisting, crying violently. For a moment the clasp of his arm, the touch of gentle sympathy, soothed and comforted her. For one wild moment she longed to confide in him, to tell him the reality. What would happen? Was it possible that Ahmed would pardon her, and let her go to her own life, her own love and lover! No, it was not possible - any other offence but this; theft or murder he could have forgiven and sheltered, but this, no! Instinctively she knew and felt it would not be possible to him - a Turk, free from prejudice and superstition, liberal as he was - to forgive her crime. Death for herself and Murad was the best she could expect. Ahmed's own honour, the traditions of all his house, his great position would make it impossible for him to let her pass from his, a Turk's harem to a Druze lover. The thought whirled from her sick brain, leaving all confused and hopeless as before, and her tears rained fast. Ahmed smoothed her soft hair and kissed her forehead gently, as it lay against his breast.

"Go and fetch your music, and sing to me," he whispered, as her sobs ceased. "See how lovely the spring time is; it is no time for tears, but for songs and - love." He murmured the last word very softly and set her free. Without looking at him she slipped away to the door in obedience to his command, and in a wild confusion of feeling in which pleasure struggled with fear.

When she came back with her instrument, a small pear shaped guitar in appearance, she was more composed. Her eyes were still red and swollen, but the soft, elastic skin had already regained its colouring. As she entered, soft bars of sunlight were falling through the room, the window had been opened, and the song of the birds came gaily through it. Ahmed had ordered coffee and sweetmeats to be brought, and these now stood on a small inlaid table before her, on whose glistening arabesques of mother of pearl the sunbeams twinkled merrily. Ahmed's eyes lighted up with tender pleasure as he saw her enter, and she noted it. He was still sitting on the couch, and held in his hand a small green leather case - the counterpart of hundreds to be seen in the jewellers' windows in Paris. Dilama guessed at once it was some present for her. Unconsciously the light, gay, butterfly nature of the girl began to reassert itself in the knowledge that the final issue had not to be met then; that there was respite for her, delay; and a natural joy stirred in her looking across at Ahmed. It was something, after all, to be queen of the harem, to be wooed in gifts and smiles by its lord.

"Come here!" he said to her, and as she approached he opened the case and took from it a bracelet, a limp band of gold with a clasp of rubies and diamonds that flashed a thousand sparkling rays into the astonished eyes of the girl, accustomed only to the dull, uncut or poorly-cut gems of the East.

"How wonderful! Is it for me, really?" she exclaimed, as Ahmed took her unresisting arm and clasped the bracelet round it above the elbow, where it lent a new beauty to the flesh.

"Now, take some coffee, and then you shall play to me while I rest and smoke," continued Ahmed, kissing her tenderly between the eyes, as she gazed up gratefully to him, and though she flushed and trembled, this time she did not shrink from him.

The coffee seemed more delicious than any that was served in the haremlik, and the gold-tipped cigarettes and the jam, made out of rose leaves, that Ahmed pressed upon her, delighted her senses and helped to make her think less of the passing hour and Murad, who would be waiting in stormy passion for her, in the angle of the wall. "I can't help it; I can't help it!" she thought to herself as she took up her instrument and bent over the strings to tune them, while Ahmed stretched himself at full length on the divan to listen, with a scarlet cushion supporting his regal head. She could both sing and play well, for Ahmed loved music, and wisely considered it a safe amusement - an outlet for superfluous passions and unexpressed feelings - for the women of the harem. Instruments were provided in plenty, and instruction and all encouragement given to them to learn, and from her first day in the harem Dilama's natural voice and talents had been noted and fostered. This afternoon, at first she was timid, and sang and played stiffly, carefully, with a great attention to notes and strings; but slowly the calm and stillness of the beautiful sun-filled room, the scented air floating in from the garden, the tense atmosphere of passion about her, and the magic beauty of the face and form opposite influenced her, grew upon her, wrapped her round, and she began to sing passionately, ardently, with that abandonment, without which all music is a hollow sound. Her glorious voice, fresh, youthful, clear, and pure came rushing joyously over her lips and filled the room. Her spirits rose as she realised the power she was exerting. She felt a little impatient at the thought of Murad. After all, she was a great lady, a lady of the harem of Ahmed Ali, the richest Turk in Damascus. She was dressed in delicate silks, and the jewels blazed on her arm. She was queen of the harem, and the beloved of its lord. He was most desirable to her and to all women, and, but for Murad, who seemed to stand like a black shadow between, she would have lain upon his breast with pure delight. She leant forward now, singing rapturously over the instrument pressed close to her soft breast, while her rose-hued fingers leapt among its strings; a transparent flush, delicate as the tint of a shell, glowed in her cheeks; her large, dark eyes looked straight at Ahmed, drawing in all the proud beauty of his face; her hair lay soft and thick without its veil above her brows, and one heavy tress fell forward over her shoulder to her knee. Ahmed lay watching her, his eyes filled with sombre fires, his whole soul listening to the song; and one other lay listening also, and this was Murad, crouching in the shade of the orange-tree plantation, catching with distended ears that flood of passionate melody wafted to him over the still garden, from the window of Ahmed's apartment, from the Selamlik.

When the song was finished, and the last notes had faltered softly into silence, Ahmed rose from his divan and crossed to where she sat. The room was full now of hot rosy light; the scent of the orange flowers poured in through the windows; the girl's senses grew confused and dizzy. Her cheeks were flaming with the excitement and joy and effort and passion of her singing; her eyelids were cast down, and beneath them her eyes watched, half in terror, half in a strained delight, the blue Persian slippers advancing silently over the matting on the floor towards her.

"Will Dilama stay with me to-night?"

The girl looked up, whitening to the lips, and slid to a kneeling position. Terror at the thought of infidelity to Murad filled her; he would infallibly find it out and avenge himself. Her face worked convulsively; she stretched out her hands with a gesture of despair.

"What my lord wills: I am the slave of his wishes."

Ahmed drew his level brows together, and for a moment lined the serene beauty of his forehead. He gazed at her with a steady, puzzled look, and at last a faint, half-quizzical smile relaxed his lips. What could this strange idea, this whim be, so unlike all Eastern maiden's usual fancies? He had not yet solved the riddle, nor found the clue! he would do so, but in the meantime she must be left her freedom. In all noble natures power brings with it a terrible responsibility, and the habit of stern self-control and long forbearance. Ahmed's complete power over the frightened piece of humanity before him brought upon him the necessity practically of surrender; for the Turk possesses one of the noblest and gentle natures the human race can boast of. Ahmed remained silent for a few seconds, and the girl gazed upon him with dilated, fascinated eyes. She noted in a dazed way how the dark blue robe parted on his breast and showed beneath a vest of gold silk, fastened a little to the side by a single emerald; how the column of throat towered above these, supporting the oval face and beautifully-modelled chin, and above these again, and the commanding brows, shone another solitary emerald between the folds of his turban on his forehead.

Murad began to seem like a robber depriving her of all these things. There is no fidelity in the body. Fidelity is a thing of the mind, always at war with and striving to coerce those instincts of the senses that are ever clamouring after the new and the unknown. Nature is ever driving us on to seek new mates. The mind with its trammels of affection, gratitude, pity, consideration, is ever dragging us back and seeking to tie us to the old. Nature's rule is fresh seasons, fresh mates, new hours, new loves. And he who seeks fidelity must woo the mind, for the body cannot give it, and knows not its laws.

After a minute's silence Ahmed stretched out his hand to her and raised her to her feet. His face had lost its smiles and fire; it was grave and sombre-looking now, but his voice was gentle as he answered her:

"You are free to return to the haremlik," he said; "no one has any power to coerce you. I wish you to come and go as you will." He waved his hand towards the curtain with a gesture of dismissal, and then turned away and rang a little silver bell on a table. The black slave appeared - it seemed almost instantly - before the curtain; while Dilama still stood, motionless, irresolute, with a curious sense of disappointment, mingling with relief, stealing over her. Ahmed beckoned the slave to him, and said something in a low voice Dilama did not catch, but the last sentence she overheard. "Send Soutouma to me," and without taking any further notice of Dilama, Ahmed turned back towards the divan, threw himself upon it, and drew the pipe-stand towards him.

The black slave, with a smile on her curving lips, motioned to Dilama to precede her, and Dilama, with one look flung backward to Ahmed's couch in the full sunlight of the window, passed under the heavy blue curtain out into the passage. "Send Soutouma to me!" the words went through her with a cutting feeling, as a knife dividing her flesh.

Soutouma was next to Buldoula in age and rank - a fair beauty of the harem, with soft, long, sunlit tresses, and a skin of snow.

"Yes, why not? why not?" asked Dilama wildly to herself as her feet dragged along down the passage side by side with the grinning black's. "I am a Druze girl: I belong to Murad and to the mountains." But the insidious charm of Ahmed's personality worked on all the pulses of her body; pulses that know not fidelity, though her brain kept telling her that

Murad would be waiting for her in the garden. But that night Murad did not come. The garden stood cool and fragrant, full of perfume and rosy light, full of the music of birds and the tints of a thousand flowers - all the invitations to love, but love itself was absent. Dilama searched the garden from end to end, and walked in and out among the roses by the buttressed wall, but the garden was empty and silent. She was alone. Tired at last, and ready to cry with fatigue and disappointment, she sat down by the red brick wall, leaning her chin on her hand and gazing up towards the windows of the Selamlik, which could only be seen in portions here and there through a leafy screen of plane-tree branches. How still it was in the garden, and how the scent of the orange flower weighed on the senses! How clear the pink, transparent air!

Through that same lucid air, under the spreading plane-trees, and through the great dim bazaars of the city, walked Murad that evening with quick, hot feet, and the liquid coursing in his veins seemed fire instead of blood. He went from Druze to Druze, wherever he could find them, in their own homes, or sitting at a shady corner of a street, where the tiny rush-bottomed stools are gathered round the tea-stalls with their hissing brazen urns and porcelain cups, or lounging in the bazaars, or at the marble drinking-fountains. Wherever they were he found them, and spoke a few hot, eager words to them, urging them to hurry forward their preparations, and be ready to start with the caravan at the rising of the full moon. Then, as the rosy light changed into violet dusk, he went home to his low, yellow, square-roofed dwelling on the edge of the desert, and sat there in his one unlighted room - sat there gazing out with unseeing eyes into the lustrous Damascus night beyond the open door, and with the fingers of his right hand playing absently with the handle of his knife.

A week had passed over and Ahmed had not sent again for Dilama, nor had Murad visited the garden, and to the Eastern girl it seemed as if the world had stopped still. The hot, languid days, the gorgeous nights with the blaze of the stars and the rapture of the nightingales, filled her with madness that seemed insupportable. She knew of no reason for Murad's desertion. She could find out nothing. She did not dare to breathe a word to any one of the anxiety, the wonder, the desperation that seemed choking her. What had become of him? What had happened? Would he ever come again? And as he appealed only to her senses, and he was not there, she ceased to wish for him very much, but thought more of Ahmed and the Selamlik that were close to her. For the mind and the imagination love in absence and long after the absent one, but the senses are stirred by proximity, and turn to the one who is nearest.

One evening, when the soft sky was a clear crimson and the full moon rose a perfect disk of transparent silver, faint as yet in the blood-red glow, Dilama felt as if she could exist no longer in the still, even, unchanging peace of the women's apartments. The song of the water without, the coo of the doves, the incessantly repeated love-note of the mating sparrows, seemed to madden her beyond endurance.

She lay face downwards on the soft carpet of her little sleeping-chamber, and moaned unconsciously aloud, "Let me die! Let me die! I have lost favour with all men."

The black slave was sitting cross-legged just outside the curtain, and when these slow, long drawn-out words came from the other side a light gleamed in her shrewd, beady-black eyes. With one claw-like hand she cautiously drew back a fold of the curtain, and peering in saw the foremost lady of the harem lying prostrate, her face pressed to the floor. She made no sound, but dropping the curtain noiselessly, sidled slowly off down the dark passage leading to the Selamlik. Ahmed was alone in his apartment when the slave appeared, sitting on the broad window ledge gazing out from the window which overlooked his grounds, and beyond them the white minarets and shining cupolas of the city. He turned at the interruption, but his face lighted up with pleasure as he recognised the women's attendant, and he signed to her to approach.

"The Lady Dilama is weeping in her chamber, desiring my lord," announced the slave, with much bowing and prostration, but still with that confidence which showed she knew how welcome the news would be to her august listener. Ahmed rose, a fire of joy leaping up suddenly within him.

"It is well," he said, in an even tone. "Let the Lady Dilama come to me, and for yourself take this," and he dropped beside the crouching heap of black back and shoulder a small velvet bag. The slave grabbed it and put it in her breast, muttering a thousand thanks and blessings, and withdrew.

Once outside, her lean black legs carried her swiftly back to Dilama's room, where she pushed aside the curtain without ceremony.

"Come!" she said imperiously, "you are Ahmed Ali's chosen one; he has sent for you. Put off that torn veil, and all that weeping. I have new robes here for you."

Dilama, who had hurriedly gathered herself up at the slave's entry, shrank away now into a corner of the room, white as death.

"Has he sent for me?" she asked breathlessly. "Commanded me? Oh, must I go?"

The slave looked at her strangely. She had no suspicion of Dilama's secret, and had no idea that her own misrepresentations were as gross as they were. But she had no wish to be harsh or unkind to this girl, who would be in a few hours queen of the harem. She was puzzled. She drew near to Dilama's shrinking form, and peered into her face.

"Yes, he *commands*," she said; "but is it possible you do not wish to go to Ahmed? He is a king amongst men, and he loves you. What better fate could there be than to lie on his breast, in his arms? Is it not better than the ground to which you were crying just now? Surely you will reward me well to-morrow?"

Dilama answered nothing. Long shivers were passing through her. It was decided, then; she could no longer avoid her fate, and already with that thought the Oriental calm of acceptance came to her. Besides, where was Murad? She could not tell. Fate had taken him from her, perhaps - the same Fate that gave her to Ahmed. She was helpless. She had no choice but to obey. And the words of the slave, accompanied by those piercing, meaning looks, inflamed her senses. After that unbearable week of solitude the summons came to her not all unwelcome, and the supreme thought of Ahmed himself loomed up suddenly, bringing irresistible joy with it. A flame passed over her cheeks; she caught the slave's skinny black hand between her own rose-leaf palms.

"Yes, I will reward you," she murmured. "Dress me beautifully, decorate me that I may find favour with Ahmed."

The slave laughed meaningly.

"Does the desert traveller burn and sigh after water, and then do the springs of Damascus not find favour in his eyes?" she asked, and laughed again as she approached Dilama, and began to undress her. In a few minutes the whole of the haremlik was in a state of pleasant excitement. The news of the dressing of the bride spread into its furthest corners, and the women came to talk and jest, and the servants fled hither and thither upon errands. Dilama was led into the large general room, and there bathed from head to foot with warm rose-water; while the others sat round and chatted together, and admired her ivory skin, with the wild rose Syrian bloom upon it, and her masses of gold-tinted chestnut hair. And the black slave bathed and anointed and dressed her with the utmost care and great self-importance, and sent the underslaves flying in all directions, one to gather syringa, and other heavy-scented blossoms from the garden, and another to fetch the jewels for her neck; and as the attar of rose bottle was found to be empty, a slave was sent with flying feet to the bazaar to purchase more; and Dilama, excited and elated, surrounded by jest and laughter and smiling faces, felt her youth leap up within her, and rejoice at coming into its kingdom - love.

In the bazaar the slave sped to the perfume-seller, and, swelling with the importance of his mission, stayed a moment to chatter with the dealer.

"They are dressing a new bride for my master, and I must hasten back," he gossiped, lounging on the merchant's little stall. "Ahmed Ali awaits her in the Selamlik; I must be going. They say her beauty is wonderful; she is not a Turk, but a Syrian from the mountains by Beirut. I must hasten: they will be waiting."

"Yes, hasten on your way," returned the perfume-seller. He was a Turk, dignified and gracious, and of no mind to listen to gossip from the harem, of which it was little short of scandalous to speak so publicly. He had other customers in his shop who could hear, amongst them a black-browed Druze in a green turban, who was waiting patiently his turn, and who seemed to listen intently to this most improper gossip. The slave disappeared with flying feet to catch up his wasted moments, but when the Turk turned to serve the silent Druze, he, too, had vanished, and some white-turbaned Arabs pressed forward in his place.

* * * * *

Dilama in her lighted chamber, with her fresh young eyes a little painted beneath their lids, and heavy gold chains about her soft young throat, sat looking into the little French mirror of cheap glass and gilt, and waiting for the attar of rose to be poured on her shining hair.

At last the boy returned breathless, and the precious stuff was poured on her hair and hands. Then she stood up radiant and the women sighed and smiled by turns as she went out, preceded by the old slave. A long narrow passage, lighted overhead by swinging coloured lamps, divided the women's from the men's apartments, and through this they passed noiselessly over the matting-covered floor. At the end fell heavy curtains, concealing the door and some steps. Here the slave left the girl, and Dilama went through the curtains alone. She mounted the steps and passed through the door. All was quite silent here, and the passage unlighted, except that through a tiny window high up above her head a streak of moonlight fell across her way. Dilama paused oppressed, she knew not by what feeling. Only a short passage and another curtained door divided her now from Ahmed's presence. Her breath came fast, her pulses beat nervously, and her feet dragged; slowly and unwillingly she crept onward, harassed by cold, vague fears. Before the door itself she trembled, and her soft hands and wrists hardly availed to push it open. It yielded slowly, and fell to behind her in silence.

The room was full of light; a silver blaze of moonlight illumined it from end to end. The great windows, over which usually the curtains were drawn, stood uncovered and wide open to the soft Damascus air. The scent of roses and jessamine from the great man's garden stole in with the silver light. The girl paused when just over the threshold: she was cold and frightened, and her body shook. Ahmed did not move or speak. He was sitting sideways to one great window, with his head resting against the high back of the one European chair that the room possessed. The light was so strong that the rich, deep blue of the turban was distinctly visible in it, but his face was in shadow. She could see, however, the noble throat and pose of the shoulders as he sat waiting. The girl's heart beat with a little sense of pleasure as she looked. Her feet crept slowly a little farther into the room. A great tide of pleasure was really just outside her heart, and would have rushed in and overwhelmed it in waves of joy had she but opened her heart's doors to it; but the shadow of Murad was on the bolts and locks, and she felt afraid. The silence and great silver light in the room oppressed her. Ahmed had not heard her enter, and had not stirred nor looked at her. She crept a little closer. The beauty of the majestic figure called her irresistibly. She drew closer. She had passed one window now, and was near enough to see the jewels flash on the slender hand that hung over the chair-arm, and the glistening light on the embroidered Turkish slippers on his feet. Shading her brow with one hand, Dilama came forward, fell at those feet and kissed them. Still there was no movement, no sound. This was so unlike Ahmed's way of treating his slaves, that the girl, forgetting her fears, looked up in sheer surprise. Then her heart seemed to stop suddenly, and then leap with excessive thuds of horror against her breast. The face above her·seemed carved in stone, pale, bloodless, calm; it was set, as the girl realised in a moment of terror and agony, in a repose that would never be broken. The large, dark eyes, still open, gazed past her, sightless, changeless. Fear, her fear of him, her awe, her oppressed terror fell from her, giving way to an infinite regret, a sorrow, a sense of loss that rushed over her, filling every cell, every atom of her being. She, the unwilling, the reluctant, the slow-coming, the grudging bride, now stood free. The bridegroom asked of her nothing, demanded nothing, needed nothing, desired nothing.

The slave-girl neither shrieked nor fainted. A great, convulsive sob tore itself from her trembling body as she rose from her knees and bent over the sitting figure. Wildly she passed her soft, shaking fingers across his brow, still warm, and round his throat, seeking mechanically the wound; then her eyes fell on the gold silk of his tunic, and just over the left breast she saw a little brown patch, and on the left side of the chair the silver light gleamed on a small, dark-red pool. He had been stabbed as he sat there, waiting for her - stabbed from the back, and the dagger thrust through to the little brown spot in the front of the tunic. And through that tiny door his life had gone.

Lying at his feet, Dilama sobbed uncontrollably, rolling her head, with its wonderful crown of flower-decked hair, and her pink-silk clad body amongst the rugs on the floor. What was the worth or use of anything now, silk or bridal attire, or beauty, or flower-decked hair? Never would any of them now be mirrored in his eyes again. Never could anything change that awful serenity, that implacable silence, out of which she felt her own love, her own desire rush upon her and devour her. Ahmed had been hers and she had shrunk from him, and now all the blood in her body she would have given willingly to replace that little scarlet stream that had borne away his life.

As she lay there, weeping in an agony of despair, a dark shadow suddenly grew in the window, and fell a black patch in the panel of white light upon the floor. A lithe figure balanced a moment on the ledge of the open window, then leapt with the silent elastic bound of a cat into the room. Dilama sprang from the floor to her knees with a smothered cry of terror.

"Murad! why have you come here?"

The Druze leant over her and caught her arm fiercely.

"To claim my own. It is not the first visit I have made to-night, as you see," and as he dragged her up from her knees he indicated the motionless figure beside them.

"You killed him!" she whispered, gazing up with dilated, terrified eyes.

"Who should, if not I? Had he not taken my wife? Come, we must be going."

With the nail-like grip on her arm, and the low, savage tones in her ears, and the blazing eyes like a tiger's, inflamed with the lust of murder above her, the girl felt sick and half-fainting with fear and misery.

"He did not take me. I was always faithful, Murad. I love you. I -" she stammered.

"It is well," returned Murad with a grim smile, "and these tears I suppose are because I was too long absent? It is true I have been some time: I had much to do, and then I knew I was quite safe, now I had settled all accounts with him. Come! the caravan is ready; the camels wait for you."

He dragged her towards the open square, the great square of the window. Without, the night-flies and the moths danced in the silver beams, the trees rose motionless and stately in the sultry air, the gracious hours moved on with all the tranquil splendour of the Oriental night. The girl threw her eyes over the sitting figure, unmoved by all the strenuous passions fighting round it. Wildly, in despairing agony, she stretched out her arms towards it in a vain, unconscious passionate appeal.

The Druze struck them downwards, and gripping her unresisting body more tightly, he leapt from the window to the slight wooden staircase without, and, like a tiger with his prey, crept away stealthily through the silver silence of the rose garden towards the desert.

Choose from Thousands of 1stWorldLibrary Classics By

A. M. Barnard
Ada Leverson
Adolphus William Ward
Aesop
Agatha Christie
Alexander Aaronsohn
Alexander Kielland
Alexandre Dumas
Alfred Gatty
Alfred Ollivant
Alice Duer Miller
Alice Turner Curtis
Alice Dunbar
Ambrose Bierce
Amelia E. Barr
Amory H. Bradford
Andrew Lang
Andrew McFarland Davis
Andy Adams
Anna Sewell
Annie Besant
Annie Hamilton Donnell
Annie Payson Call
Annonaymous
Anton Chekhov
Arnold Bennett
Arthur Conan Doyle
Arthur M. Winfield
Arthur Ransome
Atticus
B.H. Baden-Powell
B. M. Bower
Baroness Emmuska Orczy
Baroness Orczy
Basil King
Bayard Taylor
Ben Macomber
Bertha Muzzy Bower
Bjornstjerne Bjornson
Booth Tarkington
Boyd Cable
Bram Stoker
C. Collodi
C. E. Orr
C. M. Ingleby
Carolyn Wells
Catherine Parr Traill
Charles A. Eastman
Charles Dickens

Charles Dudley Warner
Charles Farrar Browne
Charles Ives
Charles Kingsley
Charles Klein
Charles Amory Beach
Charles Hanson Towne
Charles Lathrop Pack
Charles Whibley
Charles Willing Beale
Charlotte M. Braeme
Charlotte M. Yonge
Charlotte Perkins Stetson
Clair W. Hayes
Clarence Day Jr.
Clarence E. Mulford
Clemence Housman
Confucius
Cornelis DeWitt Wilcox
Cyril Burleigh
D. H. Lawrence
Daniel Defoe
David Garnett
Dinah Craik
Don Carlos Janes
Donald Keyhoe
Dorothy Kilner
Dougan Clark
Douglas Fairbanks
E. Nesbit
E.P.Roe
E. Phillips Oppenheim
Earl Barnes
Edgar Rice Burroughs
Edith Van Dyne
Edith Wharton
Edward J. O'Biren
Edward S. Ellis
Edwin L. Arnold
Eleanor Atkins
Eliot Gregory
Elizabeth Gaskell
Elizabeth McCracken
Elizabeth Von Arnim
Ellem Key
Emerson Hough
Emilie F. Carlen
Emily Dickinson
Enid Bagnold

Enilor Macartney Lane
Erasmus W. Jones
Ernie Howard Pie
Ethel Turner
Ethel Watts Mumford
Eugenie Foa
Eugene Wood
Eustace Hale Ball
Evelyn Everett-green
Everard Cotes
F. H. Cheley
F. J. Cross
Federick Austin Ogg
Ferdinand Ossendowski
Francis Bacon
Francis Darwin
Frances Hodgson Burnett
Frances Parkinson Keyes
Frank Gee Patchin
Frank Harris
Frank Jewett Mather
Frank L. Packard
Frank V. Webster
Frederic Stewart Isham
Frederick Trevor Hill
Frederick Winslow Taylor
Friedrich Kerst
Friedrich Nietzsche
Fyodor Dostoyevsky
G.A. Henty
G.K. Chesterton
Gabrielle E. Jackson
Garrett P. Serviss
Gaston Leroux
George A. Warren
George Ade
Geroge Bernard Shaw
George Durston
George Ebers
George Eliot
George Gissing
George MacDonald
George Meredith
George Orwell
George Sylvester Viereck
George Tucker
George W. Cable
George Wharton James
Gertrude Atherton

Grace E. King
Grace Gallatin
Grant Allen
Guillermo A. Sherwell
Gulielma Zollinger
Gustav Flaubert
H. A. Cody
H. B. Irving
H.C. Bailey
H. G. Wells
H. H. Munro
H. Irving Hancock
H. Rider Haggard
H. W. C. Davis
Hamilton Wright Mabie
Hans Christian Andersen
Harold Avery
Harold McGrath
Harriet Beecher Stowe
Harry Houidini
Helent Hunt Jackson
Helen Nicolay
Hendrik Conscience
Hendy David Thoreau
Henri Barbusse
Henrik Ibsen
Henry Adams
Henry Ford
Henry Frost
Henry James
Henry Jones Ford
Henry Seton Merriman
Henry W Longfellow
Herbert A. Giles
Herbert N. Casson
Herman Hesse
Homer
Honore De Balzac
Horace Walpole
Horatio Alger Jr.
Howard Pyle
Howard R. Garis
Hugh Lofting
Hugh Walpole
Humphry Ward
Ian Maclaren
Inez Haynes Gillmore
Irving Bacheller
Israel Abrahams
Ivan Turgenev
J.G.Austin

J. Henri Fabre
J. M. Barrie
J. Macdonald Oxley
J. S. Fletcher
J. S. Knowles
J. Storer Clouston
Jack London
Jacob Abbott
James Allen
James Andrews
James Baldwin
James DeMille
James Joyce
James Lane Allen
James Lane Allen
James Oliver Curwood
James Oppenheim
James Otis
James R. Driscoll
Jane Austen
Janet Aldridge
Jens Peter Jacobsen
Jerome K. Jerome
John Burroughs
John Cournos
John F. Kennedy
John Gay
John Glasworthy
John Habberton
John Joy Bell
John Kendrick Bangs
John Milton
John Philip Sousa
Jonas Lauritz Idemil Lie
Jonathan Swift
Joseph A. Altsheler
Joseph Carey
Joseph Conrad
Joseph E. Badger Jr
Joseph Hergesheimer
Joseph Jacobs
Jules Vernes
Julian Hawthrone
Julie A Lippmann
Justin Huntly McCarthy
Kakuzo Okakura
Kenneth Grahame
Kenneth McGaffey
Kate Langley Bosher
Kate Langley Bosher
Katherine Cecil Thurston

Katherine Stokes
L. A. Abbot
L. T. Meade
L. Frank Baum
Latta Griswold
Laura Lee Hope
Laurence Housman
Lawrence Beasley
Leo Tolstoy
Leonid Andreyev
Lewis Carroll
Lewis Sperry Chafer
Lilian Bell
Lloyd Osbourne
Louis Hughes
Louis Tracy
Louisa May Alcott
Lucy Fitch Perkins
Lucy Maud Montgomery
Lydia Miller Middleton
Lyndon Orr
M. Corvus
M. H. Adams
Margaret E. Sangster
Margaret Vandercook
Margret Penrose
Maria Edgeworth
Maria Thompson Daviess
Mariano Azuela
Marion Polk Angellotti
Mark Overton
Mark Twain
Mary Austin
Mary Catherine Crowley
Mary Cole
Mary Hastings Bradley
Mary Roberts Rinehart
Mary Rowlandson
M. Wollstonecraft Shelley
Maud Lindsay
Max Beerbohm
Myra Kelly
Nathaniel Hawthrone
Nicolo Machiavelli
O. F. Walton
Oscar Wilde
Owen Johnson
P.G. Wodehouse
Paul and Mabel Thorne
Paul G. Tomlinson
Paul Severing

Percy Brebner
Peter B. Kyne
Plato
R. Derby Holmes
R. L. Stevenson
R. S. Ball
Rabindranath Tagore
Rahul Alvares
Ralph Bonehill
Ralph Henry Barbour
Ralph Victor
Ralph Waldo Emmerson
Rene Descartes
Rex Beach
Rex E. Beach
Richard Harding Davis
Richard Jefferies
Richard Le Gallienne
Robert Barr
Robert Frost
Robert Gordon Anderson
Robert L. Drake
Robert Lansing
Robert Lynd
Robert Michael Ballantyne
Robert W. Chambers
Rosa Nouchette Carey
Rudyard Kipling
Samuel B. Allison

Samuel Hopkins Adams
Sarah Bernhardt
Sarah C. Hallowell
Selma Lagerlof
Sherwood Anderson
Sigmund Freud
Standish O'Grady
Stanley Weyman
Stella Benson
Stephen Crane
Stewart Edward White
Stijn Streuvels
Swami Abhedananda
Swami Parmananda
T. S. Ackland
T. S. Arthur
The Princess Der Ling
Thomas A. Janvier
Thomas A Kempis
Thomas Anderton
Thomas Bailey Aldrich
Thomas Bulfinch
Thomas De Quincey
Thomas H. Huxley
Thomas Hardy
Thomas More
Thornton W. Burgess
U. S. Grant
Valentine Williams

Various Authors
Vaughan Kester
Victor Appleton
Virginia Woolf
Walter Camp
Walter Scott
Washington Irving
Wilbur Lawton
Wilkie Collins
Willa Cather
Willard F. Baker
William Dean Howells
William le Queux
W. Makepeace Thackeray
William W. Walter
Winston Churchill
Yei Theodora Ozaki
Yogi Ramacharaka
Young E. Allison
Zane Grey